Wallwave the Sea King
ADVENTURES OF WAR QUEENS AND BATTLE HEROES

In the days before written history, clues to everyday events can be found of the existence of a chariot-based civilization in the Western Plains of Russia and Mongolia. This pointed to a way of life based on chariots, horses and bronze-age weapons. These clues included the aerial sites, chariots, jewelry, swords and axes. Evidently the charioteers lived, died and were buried in a horse-based way of life that was more advanced in terms of chariots that had been developed up to that time.

This civilization had apparently covered much of the Asian and the Chinese as well as the Russian Western Plains. It was a pre-Celtic way of life. We do not know the name of the tribes or what language they spoke. The islands and rivers had not yet been taken over by Vikings, as happened later. How did a pre-Viking and pre-Celtic civilization develop into the later domination of the Vikings which was spread throughout eastern Europe and western Asia and Russia?

Obviously, pre-Gaelic and pre-Viking legends and myth need to be consulted. The longboats of war as well as chariots play a powerful part in these adventures. In those days the warrior queens as well as heroic Vikings played a large part.

The latter-day wars organized by Queen Bodicea of Britain who drove the Romans out of the British Isles; Queen Maeve of Connaught who led the united armies of Ireland against Ulster were similarly heroic figures. These warrior queens were field-marshals and planners of war as well as chariot warriors. Perhaps the last of this line was Saint Joan of Arc.

In WALLWAVE THE SEA KING, the wicked War Queen Snakeknife tries to complete her plans of conquest with the help of the Four Witches of Kill and their magic.

Wallwave the Sea King
TWISTED PATHS TO THE ROUND SEA

This story is full of the intrigues and onslaughts of the Hillwolf King Warchariot and his wicked War Queen Snakeknife who try to overcome Wallwave the Sea King and conquer the world.

LIFE OF DREW CARSON

Sam Drew Carson was born in the North of Ireland and educated there at Wellington College and the Ulster Polytechnic. He completed his education in the USA at New Mexico Highlands University and the University of Arkansas and has traveled widely in North America, around the Atlantic and in Europe.

Drew worked as a seaman and fish-gutter in Vestmannaeyjar off the coast of Iceland. He lived and worked in the Irish and Western Isles Gaeltachts and was married in Welsh-speaking Carmarthen after which he honeymooned in Belfast. He has told his stories, composed and sung his songs, seeking storylines in Bristol and the English Westcountry. Drew has also lived and written in Nashville, Tennessee, in the wooded hills of Mid-America and from the Appalachians to the Ozarks. This was the culture that gave rise to the now worldwide Scotch-Irish country music.

In the USA, he also worked beside the bayous of the French-speaking Cajuns in the South and among the Western Spanish-speaking Navajos, Apaches and Pueblos of the Sangre de Cristo Mountains in New Mexico.

Drew has sailed far into the seas of old Gaelic and Oriental legend. After many years searching for inspiration for story and music, the author is still traveling and writing.

BOOKS BY THE SAME AUTHOR

Wallwave the Sea King

Adventures of War Queens and Battle Heroes

By
Drew Carson

Order from:
https://www.createspace.com/3980869

Legals

ISBN: 978-1-908184-05-4

CONTENTS

MAIN CHARACTERS IN
THE ADVENTURES OF WALLWAVE

SEAGULL HEROES – THE WAVEWARRIORS

Waterbear, *King of Seagulls, an oriental warrior. Rider of the Great White Stallion (a horse with white hair and mane)*

Seaspear, *admiral of the Hillwolves fleet, a fieldmarshal of the sea of Wavewarrior origin*

Stormleaper, *a hero of many battles*

Whaleroarer, *a hero of fierce combats*

Icedragon, *a hero and fieldmarshal deputy*

Summersailor, *vice-king and fieldmarshal supreme, head of Hawks battalion*

Shadowhero, *great uncle and trainer of the young*

Wallwave,* *oriental youth, son of Waterbear*

Stormbolt, *younger son of Waterbear*

also known as Tsunami

HILLWOLVES

Warchariot, *King of Hillwolves*

Sternrider, *supreme fieldmarshal and commander in chief of Hillwolves. Rider of the Great Bay Horse of the West*

Winterwarrior, *deputy fieldmarshal and next in command of the Hillwolves*

Winterfire, *the son of Winterwarrior*

Oakhill, *an assassin*

Cragfox, *in charge of shoreline defenses*

MAIN CHARACTERS

Flyingbat, *brother of Oakhill*
Abbott Ratrunner, *a monk who breeds rats*

The Deathhead Dwarfs, *four-eyed assassins*
The Killer Disguisers, *chamelion-like killers*

HILLWOLF QUEENS

Queen Snakeknife, *queen of Warchariot*
Queen Spiderlair, *Warchariot's ancient mother*
Queen of Justice, *a sycophant, a false omenteller*
Queen Rainbow, *Snakeknife's mother*

SEAGULL QUEENS

Springvision, *queen of Waterbear. She has the gifts of magic and spells and discernment of spirits*
Gentleleaf, *loyal queen of Seaspear*
Whitehair, *young niece of Summersailor*
Purplelake, *sister of Summersailor*
Maplewine, *queen to Whaleroarer*
Willowflame, *queen to Icedragon*
Streamflower, *queen to Stormleaper*

FOUR WITCHES OF KILL

Windweasel, *of the air*
Rivershark, *of the waters*
Meteoreyes, *of fire and hills*
Landslink, *of soil and earth*

MAIN CHARACTERS

TWO STALLIONS
Oceanhorse, *the Great White Stallion of the East*
Foresthorse, *the Great Bay Stallion of the West*

SUPERNATURALS
Truthteller, *Master of good words*
Washerwoman, *Diviner of omens*
Mooncrow, *a spy-bird of war*
Red Warriorwoman, *teller of fortunes*
Bullaxe, *ugly ogre with magic powers*
Firefiend, *a man of flames*
Tear, Sigh, Smile, Laugh, *Queens from Islands of the Everyoung*

COMBAT PERSONA
Salmon of Wisdom
Wine of Vision
*Shield of Roar, gives warning
*Bonespear, thirsts for blood
*Hardblade, a rainbow sword
magic weapons that occasionally appear

CHAPTER ONE
TWO ARMIES WAIT

Wallwave the new King of the Wavewarriors sat high on his fastness overlooking the sea. He had just been given many words of wisdom from his council, his fieldmarshals and their war queens.

Then he sent out brightly colored birds that bore a message to his distant islands. "Come to us now. We need your help to build up our fleet against the cruel armies of our enemies, the Hillwolves. They gather up their arms and accoutrements of war against us to destroy us. Sail to us speedily for we have been disrupted with warwords and all our ships and heroes have been turmoiled. Sail to our lough with all your ships and seamen."

The small talking birds flew far, far away to speak this message to the scattered Seagulls. For nine long days Wallwave pondered what to do.

***

As dolphins and small birds played far out at sea, a fleet of small light fast-flowing longboats, caravels and rowing boats with smooth white sails, rowed into view over the round horizon. Oars with hard blades and stiff shafts dipped together, pulled by stern oarsmen rising and falling forward, strongly and eagerly, as they sped the many long small ships over the main.

Steady in time and regular, they left a frothy, spraying and foamy wake flowing behind the boats like white-haired horses. Great was the pomp and pride of those foam-horses. Their tails and manes flowed out and shone and tossed over the slow blue waves in billowy crests.

At the front of the boats, the eager and ever leaning-forward long-necked prows of the proud and searching skiffs were like hungry snakeheads rasping and snapping.

When King Wallwave saw the fleet on the horizon he took the form of a yellow, widewinged seabird and flew over the fleet to find out whether they were friends come to support him or enemies.

So Wallwave spread his wings over the fleet and blackened out the sun. Then a savage storm arose in the sky below the wings of Wallwave. The dark clouds brooded slowly over the sea just like the misty pall that drapes a palace when a king draws near to it on a winter's night.

The fleet cringed low from the Wallwave's wings, as the winds brewed and the waves leapt high in fear, and the mermaids screamed as their hair streamed out in terror. The small birds and the seagulls screeched in madness. And the green seaweeded waves were in an uproar as the cold waters stirred in anger and in hatred.

The birds that hovered overhead were insane as they attacked each other and threw themselves upon the barks and boats. The ropes all strained and stretched and the woods of the boats groaned.

The crossbeams creaked and the sails ripped in the rain. The masts shivered and cried and tore in two as the shadow of the Wallwave fell upon them. The ribs of many ships were battered and broken. The gear swept overboard as men clung to the sides. Even the nails in the woods withered and shuddered and some of the sailing craft were overturned as the hulls of the boats swept floating over the masts.

The nearby rocks moaned and wept in the bitter blasts.

But the Wallwave saw no foe among the fleet and folded his great wings like an albatross and glided to the shore of his own island.

The storm grew calm with the blue waves lapping mildly. The winds grew tame like birds within their nests and the seas flowed gently by coves and rocks and harbor.

Then the sea became a friendly tide of passage as the great fleet came ashore in shouts of triumph. No one had need to row or sail in turmoil as their sails filled out with the warm winds of travel as the sea led them ashore to join their new King Wallwave.

The first boat was filled with ugly men of war with close-cropped hair, faces of warts and scars. Loudmouthed they were, sweating, hard-bodied and fierce as they were heard yelling for the blood of Warchariot and his War Queen

Snakeknife. They spat and cursed and cried, Revenge for brave Waterbear.

The largest of the longboats held a champion, for at its prow stood the bravest of the brave. A herolight shone all about that warrior. A halo of fire and brightness flashed around him.

War Queen Whitehair stood on the ramparts and cried out to her ladies, "See in that prow there stands a straight and tall man. His cheeks are red as blood, his skin is yellow, his brows are gray, his eyes gray-blue. His hair is long and wavy, white as snow. His frown is like the snarling of a tiger. Heart of stone! That is the Icedragon come back."

The Icedragon strode ashore to shouts of joy from those who loved his coming.

The Wallwave, now returned to his human form, welcomed the hero, "I thank you Icedragon for these men and ships. We need you and we need these tough sea fighters who all have now survived a short storm trial."

The Icedragon replied, "I scanned the seas and I led away as many as would follow. So, here are 200 ships all filled and furious with rebels against the Warchariot and Snakeknife."

Later King Wallwave took his throne on the high roof and looked out at the longboats of Icedragon, for the ships had been hauled ashore to be fixed and fitted, armed and redecked and roped like a fleet of war.

Around the ramparts sat the heroes, Icedragon, Whaleroarer and Stormleaper. In the centre, on pillows of seabirds' down and woolen cushions, War Queen Whitehair reclined as tall and graceful as a swan. Seated around her were the three ladies-in-waiting: the yellow Streamflower, the dark red Maplewine and Willowflame, like a willow tree on fire.

Then the Icedragon told of his adventures since he had gone away from the Inn of Warwords to join the treasonous deserter, Summersailor.

"When Summersailor invited me to join him, I refused but offered to go with the Hawkarmy to train and protect them.   I asked Summersailor for his sure guarantee of my neutrality.   He gave me this protection in the hope that I would change my mind and join him later.

"However, such strange events and sights and such dark omens took place that Summersailor almost led the Hawks back to our side but he did not do so or lead them from the weird killers of the Hillwolves.

"I followed Summersailor to the castle of the Warchariot and his War Queen Snakeknife. I saw and met the cruelest murderers of the Hillwolves. These are the ones who kill by subterfuge, by trickery and by treachery and by poison.

"They have some powerful battle heroes too but most are those who kill by patient cunning and go out into the world as hired assassins. We need to cleanse the world of these scum killers."

"And we will do so, Icedragon," said the Wallwave.

Icedragon continued on with his strange adventure tale.

"In the fastness of Warchariot and Snakeknife, where your brave earthly father was lured and killed, I saw a clan of murderous disguisers. They were all skilled in dressing to match the background of their prey - black, white, trees' bark or grass and bushes glued upon them. Three troops of three assassins were ready and waiting. The first was dressed in black over black skins, black masks, swords, shields, daggers and spears of black. This troop was ready and dressed for all the seasons. Ready for winter snows or blind midnight.

"I saw them gasping and panting like dogs for prey with black, thick, straight hair falling down to their shoulders. They wore black creeping shoes and black gloves that held black daggers.

"Some were in white for the snowdays of winter. They were silent as graves, invisible at night but deadly. They will line up at a snowy wall or at a white-covered snow bank where snow lies all around a victim's house. They will spring forward and throw themselves on their victim late at night and knife him to death from three different directions. No one will see them come, kill or escape.

"The second troop of three were dressed in bark. Weapons and bodies, headmasks, stood like trees, ready to murder in a wood or copse.

"The third troop of three were dressed in green leaves and grasses ready to kill on a sunny day. At noon the grasses shimmer and come alive. Swords and spears close in on you like walking bushes and as they come alive you scream in death.

"All three disguisers, dressed in kill regalia, sit in Warchariot's hall ready to go and to do his bidding at any time of the year. These three disguisers were one clan who had developed their killskills over the generations. Stripped of their disguises they looked alike, each one like leering death ready to strike.

"Also, there lurk in that fortress of filth, other cold killers dedicated to death. Three ugly Deathheads stalk that castle's halls. Their bodies are covered in hard scaly stone so strong that no sharp sword could ever pierce it. Spikes from their heads stick out in poisoned sharpness. If I had thrown a bushel of hard crabapples at any one of those spikeheaded monsters not a crabapple would have reached the floor, for every apple would have ended up stuck on their spikeheads.

"Each Deathhead had four black beetle eyes. The eyes were grown at front and back and at each side over the ear so that they watched and looked in all directions. Within each eye gazed seven baleful pupils.

"Their flatnosed grinning faces were like monkeys. Their bodies all were dwarfed, unclothed and hairy, strutting from side to side like mad gorillas with powerful apely hands wrinkled and knarled. In each tight hand was held an iron flail and from each flail there hung seven strong chains with sharpspiked razor thorns on every chain just like a miniature of their own spikeheads.

"All the swift Deadheads loped along the ramparts looking for enemies with their four eyes. If any intruder had been caught by them, that enemy would have been cut into fine mincemeat so small that it might well have been passed through a cornmeal sieve after the Deathhead flails had sliced with their sharp and frenzied butchery.

"And even more terrifying than those misshapen apemen were three old black-cowled killers from the pit. They walk the lower basements of the castle, summoned back from the abyss by spells and chants and sacrifices too vile for human words. These friary figures wear dark robes with long black hair falling on their shoulders. They carry swinging cages filled with rats. They are the Monks of Plague who spread disease and foulest pestilence upon their enemies, setting the rats of the black death upon them.

"These monks have cruel and ulcered hands and faces. Already dead, they cannot be killed again. Drive a sword through them and you stab the air. Cut off their heads, it is of no avail for these are shadows from the pit of turmoil.

"Centuries ago they died of the black plague and now as fiends they stalk the halls of earth in the dread caverns of the assassin's lair. Their master is the Abbot Ratrunner whose spells in laboratories spawn diseases. These monks are held in check only by spells or else they would unleash their rats and plagues on all mankind, including the Hillwolves."

King Wallwave and his War Queen Whitehair with her ladies-in-waiting together with the heroes Whaleroarer and Stormleaper were all distressed and stunned to hear of the horrors that were lying in wait at the castle of Warchariot and Snakeknife.

CHAPTER TWO
AN UNEASY KING

Wallwave thanked the Icedragon, "You have risked your life to bring us what we needed to know about the killdungeons of Warchariot and his War Queen Snakeknife. We must confront those horrors one day soon. Now, tell us about Warchariot and Snakeknife. What are their minds now focused on and how do you think they will attack us?"

***

The Icedragon shook his head and thoughtfully replied to the Wallwave, "Warchariot's sick mind is near to confusion. When I came to him, under the firm protection of Summersailor, he did not welcome any of us, but rather sent out for soothsayers, interpreters of signs, readers of omens and the like, to guide him.

"A redrobed young girl had ridden up in her chariot. She was red-skinned with three red pupils in each eye and had the gift of sure foresight.

"Under our very faces, Warchariot asked her to prophesy whether we would help or hinder in his war. He skulked and plucked his beard and scratched his face and scrutinized us. He peered at us suspiciously.

"Pointing at me and Summersailor he asked the visionary, what did she see of Icedragon the hero or Summersailor the fieldmarshal, the two generals just come to join his army and to guide him.

"The young girl had answered, 'I see blood upon them.'

"Then Snakeknife cried out, 'Of course, in a great battle the blood of enemies will splatter on our men, even on us. Yes, accidents will happen. We may even wound each other by mistake but we will win, look at our future.'

"The girl in red replied, 'I see blood on you. I see blood on your captains and your warriors. I see the crows fly down to drink your blood. I see the wild dogs crunching on your bones. You are Hillwolves. One day the dog will eat the dog.'

" 'Of course, we will have our mishaps,' cried Warchariot, 'but see, we have Summersailor and his Hawkarmy come over now to our side. Here is Icedragon. Look one more time and tell us what you see.'

" 'I see blood on you,' spoke the crimson maiden.

"Then the Summersailor spoke, 'My swift Hawkarmy was the crack division of Wallwave's hosts. Hear the mighty army of the Wavewarriors approaching like the seagulls of the sky, in winds of winter, to join us. Wallwave is but a boy and his younger brother trains with his great uncle.

" 'The Wallwave's hosts have scattered far and wide to the four corners of the earth in smallboats, here and there, in wooden skiffs, barks and coracles. They could not be battle-ready in 100 years. Now look more wisely, woman of the redeyes. You are red of skin and eyes and drive red horses.

" 'Try to discern more truly, what do you see?'

"The redwoman cracked her whip and drove off calmly, 'I see blood, Summersailor. I see blood,' she cried as she rode off.

"Snakeknife was furious and raised her spear, 'I can still transfix her.'

" 'Do not,' Warchariot told her, 'our omens are bad so let us take this warning to improve them. Killing a wise one, a strange prophetess, might bring bad luck and only make things worse.   Let us be calm and think what we must do.'

"Then the king's juggler threw up seven swords and seven apples, passing each other like bees on a summer day. The sword would cut the apples in mid-air and the apples would be caught by the juggler before they hit the ground, but now all fell upon the ground and smashed into pieces.

"Warchariot asked, 'Why now for the first time in forty years has this trick failed to work? I feel the evil eye lurking all around us.'

"Then the crows and the ravens screeched and cawed loudly in the battlements. Wild ghosts in the walls yelled out and laughed and uproared. Crocodiles ground their teeth and croaked and grinned in the filthy moats that kept the foe at bay. The stone flags of the castle shook and shifted.

" 'What is that powerful roar?' said War Queen Snakeknife as she jumped up to her feet.

"Then Warchariot drew his sword and grasped his javelin.

" 'This is my gift to you,' laughed the Winterwarrior.

" 'What kind of gift would make this castle shudder?' asked Warchariot.

"Snakeknife cried out, 'Is this some kind of joke?'

"Winterwarrior pointed his hand at the Summersailor, 'That mighty roar is the Summersailor's Hawks, the crack division of the Seagull Warriors.'

" 'No,' said Snakeknife, 'an army out of nowhere? I see you are laughing. Do not make fools of us. Surely the great seamonster that holds up the seabed has turned over on its back and split the seaswamps into seething earthquakes.'

"King Warchariot sprang outside to see the cause. Thousands of birds had landed all around the castle. Perched on rocks and sand, the white screeching seahawks were jumping up and down and fluttering their wings.

"Then hazily they changed into fierce warriors and war horses and chariots of battle. Great was the pomp and pride of the brave horses as their tails and manes shook out and shone and tossed. The warriors were dressed in tunics of leaf green with coats of mail held on by golden pins all in the shapes of seaweed animals.

"Their hair was long and flowed over their shields, round and hard-edged with cutting edge of silver. Each warrior held a gold spear and a sword. Then he rolled back the thin flexible swordblade around his wrist and then flashed it like a bangle as it unraveled and straightened out of its own accord.

"As the seahawks transformed themselves into grim warriors they became hooknosed and lean and swift and deft in all the tricks of battleready heroes. For their cloaks were speckled red and yellow like hawks. The spears on their backs were three-pointed and sharp as any beaks or talons of the predator.

"They threw their ivory-hilted swords up high into the air, then threw their silken scabbards after the swords to join them and ensheath them in the mid-air. Then they reversed the trick and threw the scabbards first then the sharp swords were thrown up and entered into the silken scabbards before they hit the ground. All the sheathed swords were caught in mid-air by the great Hawkarmy.

"Many of the Hawks' longboats and coracles were laden with swords and shields and spears and catapults. And all the accoutrements of war were piled high upon the battle chariots in the boats.

"Many men moved in unison, shoulder to shoulder and in step by step. The swords, thrown up and caught, were pointed towards the enemy in intricate and interchangeable complexity. Men shamfought hand-to-hand. Then they threw themselves into a chariot and flew to another changing scene of battle elsewhere in the wide field of the shoreline.

"Then chariots filled with swords and dirks and daggers were driven around for their comrades to select at just the one right moment in the battle when such a choice could make the difference.

"Warchariot, pleased with the new Hawkarmy, cried out, 'Each warrior fights like a hardened, seasoned fighter. He knows what he needs to do and how to do it.'

"But War Queen Snakeknife fumed with jealousy and resentment, 'It would be foolish to accept these Hawks. They would get all the credit for our victories and our own warriors would be driven to a mutiny. The Hawks would get all spoils and again our men would get but little and hate us and desert us. Let us leave these Hawks behind. I do not trust them.'

"The fieldmarshal Winterwarrior spoke up to defend the great warriors of the Hawkarmy that had joined him, 'But they are fighting for us. If we reject them they will go and fight for the other side. They might even try to seize our land when we had gone and turned our backs on them, to go to war.' Then he bowed to Warchariot.

"It was clear that Warchariot agreed with Winterwarrior. But War Queen Snakeknife still objected, 'Let us put our own commanders over them to rule them.'

"Warchariot shook his head, 'They would not follow anyone but a leader sanctioned by the Summersailor, their feared longterm fieldmarshal.'

"Snakeknife was obsessed with jealousy and cried out, 'Then let us kill them swiftly unawares. See how our archers line up on the ramparts with their arrows pointed down at this Hawkarmy. We have the advantage over them. Let us just kill them. Thus, we will never need to fight them.'

"Summersailor jumped up and pointed his finger at the Snakeknife, Queen of the Assassins. 'You will do this only over my dead body.'

" 'That is the general idea,' said the Snakeknife, grimly.

" 'That may not be so easy,' replied the Summersailor.

"Warchariot tried to calm the stirring waters. 'We are not strong enough to kill them, nor can we just send them off to help the enemy,' Warchariot had muttered.

"Snakeknife sneered in hatred of the Hawkarmy but changed her mind and ordered, 'Let us divide them up and scatter them throughout our entire army. In this way they will strengthen all our forces and even train them. Soon all our forces could be likewise skilled and just as dexterous as the great Hawkarmy. Then there will be no jealousy against them.'

"This division and redistribution was carried out and the Hawks were so divided that they formed just five percent of each battalion.

"But Summersailor pointed out, 'They will lose some tricks. For now, several cannot be gathered into one chariot and moved away to strengthen another part of our Wolfarmy. They will lack cohesion and espirit de corps.'

" 'No matter, let them be split up,' said Snakeknife.

"Then Winterwarrior reminded the Summersailor, 'You are still my deputy, my righthand man. Soon all our army will be just like yours.'

"Yet Summersailor was sad to see the breakup of the Hawkarmy, the Seagulls' crack division.

"Next dawn, when the whole army went to hunt for deer, the warriors from the crack Hawkarmy killed almost all of the deer for venison. So the jealousy of the Hawks by the Hillwolves continued on, despite the splitup of the crack division by that envious War Queen Snakeknife."

***

And when Wallwave, the Seagull king, had heard this story from the Icedragon, who told him everything, the king replied, "Icedragon, I am most pleased to know that our Hawkarmy was dispersed and broken up to appease the jealousy of a stupid queen. For now we will never need to fight them as a unit or as a fighting force, as one.

"Let troublemakers and destructive men be stood against and outlawed, even my uncle the Summersailor. We will win and overcome them, for we are Make and they are Break.

"Desertion or changing sides in warfare is to steal men and to break up what has been long created and established. This is an act of Break and not an act of Make."

The Icedragon added, "I was able to speak quietly to some of our warriors and bring them here to join us, for there were some who would not change sides to join Warchariot. These were the fighters who feared Summersailor when he had challenged them to join or leave him. They had furtived into the background in the night. They came here in the armada which I brought, along with many deserters and tax rebels who seized the chance to take up swords against War Queen Snakeknife and Warchariot."

And the Wallwave answered with a smile, ". . whom I almost destroyed with a short squall when I wallwaved on my wings of storm. That was a gift I inherited from my godfather, the Truthteller of the Darts who lives high in the sky."

***

Then birds flew out of the bushes and flocked upwards and the moon dimfaded into the light of dawn as the sun rose up out of the East like a hero. This was a new day led by the Wallwave, King of the Wavewarriors, with a fury light shining around his head and a halo of fire and brightness flashing around him.

CHAPTER THREE
SCOUTS AND SKIRMISHERS

Then Wallwave enquired of the Icedragon, "Tell us then, what is the state of the Warchariot's army of dogs compared to our Seagull Warriors?"

"They are stronger than we are," replied Icedragon, "now that our crack division serves among them. But I was never able to observe them, for I was watched by Summersailor and the viceking Winterwarrior who is the supreme fieldmarshal of the Hillwolves and also next in rank under King Warchariot. But being watched and guaranteed by all the deputies of Warchariot did not assuage the king's deep mistrust in me. Both Warchariot and Snakeknife were always suspicious and untrusting of all the Seagulls. So I could not observe and count them freely."

Wallwave nodded and agreed, "I see. I understand. So, let us go out as scouts and spies, perhaps even as skirmishers.

"All four of us will sail and infiltrate their outer flanks in secret, observe them and assess them for their numbers, their strengths and skills and vulnerabilities.

"Let us approach their camp from all directions, north and south, west and east, all the four points of the compass. We will surround them with our eyes, learn all we can and later take up the fighting in the full knowledge of where and whom we know.

"Of course there may well be petty skirmishes and we may damage them in some small ways, but let us leave the heavy fighting till later. Meanwhile our men and ships will get in shape and rebuild and arm themselves for the hard fights that lie ahead."

Whaleroarer, the Stormleaper and the Icedragon all agreed.

Then War Queen Whitehair asked Wallwave, "Let me come with my three ladies: Streamflower, Maplewine and Willowflame. Since it is only going to be for reconnaissance, we can help and besides we are skilled in many of the arts of war. So let each queen of arms go with her warrior."

But Icedragon, Stormleaper and Whaleroarer refused, saying, "There could still be setbacks and looking after ladies is a burden. While we protect them, we are in greater danger."

"Who needs protection and who is the protector?" asked War Queen Whitehair.

Then she addressed the Wallwave, pointing out, "We rescued these true heroes from foul witches. I beg you order them to take us. Who is most in need of help against mindmagic? The four witches are seen as lovely ladies only by the men, blinded by the sweet aromas of Windweasel, Rivershark, Landslink and the Meteoreyes. The four Witches of Kill can metamorphize; only we ladies can see the witches as they really are."

Wallwave smiled and nodded, "We need to know who is kind beauty, and who is a poisonous witch. You may come with us."

So the four heroes, each with his own war queen and entourage all fully dressed in battle armor and shields, sailed out to reconnoiter the enemy.

Wallwave laid his plans before the heroes, "We will sneak in from the north, south, west and east to spy on all things hidden on their island."

So, four longboats sailed out laden with chariots along with all the accoutrements of battle and swords and javelins and fine warhorses. Great was the pomp and the pride of those horseheroes as their tails and manes shook out and shone and tossed, all standing quietly in the warboats' hold.

Whitehair went with Wallwave to the East in the longboat named Truce. The Icedragon and Willowflame sailed north to the snow in the longboat, Nightbattle while the Stormleaper and Streamflower traveled south in the fast longboat known as Waterfight.

The Whaleroarer and Maplewine came by the west, sailing out in the longboat called Winningspears, by the shortest route to reach the land of caves. They sailed by night, in secret to that land of ice and wind, to the snowland where Warchariot and his cold War Queen Snakeknife had camped out their army and pitched their tents in the centre of the peninsula.

Snowhills and trees and bushes of ice gave cover to the four groups of scouts as they scanned all that lay hidden among the trees before them.

But as they landed in the four parts of the nearisland, the moon came out and walked across the sky.

The Mooncrow heard the noise of faint boats scraping. Lurking in a dark corner of the castle she stirred and stretched her blackwings and flew out to see the newcome scouts from the Wavewarriors. Mooncrow's blackwings flew; her yellow eyes peered out, her orange beak muttered and croaked.

The longboat Winningspear with Whaleroarer and Maplewine landed in a hidden cove on the west coast. Down to that cove there flowed a shallow river where the Hillwolves launched their boats to the open sea.

Then the two skirmishers and their retainers trekked inland to spy out the Wolves' west flanks.

The Whaleroarer and Maplewine left Winningspear in the hands of charioteers and able seamen.

Then Maplewine put on her coats of mail, helmet of strong steel, shield of silver, wrist enstrengtheners of thick studded linen, her knee and ankle straiteners of leather and on her back a bundle of light javelins.

She followed Whaleroarer in his full gear of war and in all his sharp accoutrements of battle along the banks of the snowy landingstream until at last they reached the hilly top and saw before them the Wolves' camps of war.

As they trekked, the Whaleroarer uprooted many trees, stripped them by hand of all the little branches and threw them into the middle riverbed. He handled each tree like a javelin so that they landed and planted rootdown and upright along the middle of the launching stream and just below the surface of the icetop.

As they trekked, the Whaleroarer explained to Maplewine, "These trees will grow into the muddy bed beneath the ice and snow. In the warm spring they will obstruct and stall the passage of the Wolves' longboats as their warriors try to launch them. There will be no space on either side for boats."

Suddenly, they had trekked to a ridge of trees and bushes, snowcovered, and overlooking the Hillwolves' camp. All the grey tents and cool pavilions of the foe stretched out across the busy field.

Gathered around one tent in a large circle were a dozen swordsmen performing tricks of swordplay. They fenced with silver swords and juggled dirks. All had huge manes of golden hair and all were of the same breadth, shape and height. It was as though they all had been cast in the same mint. Their swords were hilted with pure ivory and each tall swordsman wore a bright red tunic.

Whaleroarer pointed to a warrior, "That is the royal guard," he whispered to Maplewine and then he pointed to a tent, "and no doubt that tent is the tent of Warchariot and his war queen."

A great black cauldron brewed and bubbled there. Then out of the royal tent strode a young man, his skin as black as the brew in the black cauldron. With flaming eyes and huge powerful hands he held a three-pronged spear. This he plunged it into the boiling pot and flames shot up covering the whole spear.

"That is King Warchariot's general, Ratrunner, who is next in line to the Winterwarrior. He is preparing his poisoned spear for cunning battle."

Inside the open tent door could be seen three beautiful young girls combing their hair. All three were wearing cloaks of silk with broaches of pure gold holding all their robes together. Their hair was long and curly and shiny and yellow.

Fine maids and ladies and servants waited upon them. Beside each girl was a long burning candle, unused at present but later to be lighted, to guide their sewing and wicker craftsmanship.

Whaleroarer told Maplewine that the three young girls of beauty in the royal tent were the three nieces of the Warchariot. "Each one is promised to a king or prince. Soon they will sail away to their new loves, the princes of far countries over the sea. No doubt they will bring more land under the rule and iron grip of Snakeknife and Warchariot. For all things in their lives must serve the greed and powerlust of Snakeknife and Warchariot.

"There, moving within the tent, is a huge warrior with a head of hair like a whinbush in the spring. A heavy three-edged sword hangs at his side. His shield of bright red gold is dashed with specks of silver, riveting the strong plates together.

"There stands a sinister and angry lynx with the cold blood of greed within his breast, his body full of wounds that could not tame him nor hurt his heart of stone.

"Triumph in battles is his destiny, carved out for him at birth by the harp players who spin the wheel of fortune. A lucky man needs only to be born.

"His body was to be the dwelling of a hero. Blood of ice flows in him: skin white as snow: balanced and deft in chariot: the headwave of a coming warlike sea. That is King Warchariot. He is a like fierce mad bull and a sad implacable foe."

Maplewine looked over the cold pavilions and tried to assess the warriors around the tents, "There are two armies but one of them is small and far more highly skilled than the larger army. The small division move their chariots, their weapons and their men, from place to place, more swiftly and more surely.

"That small company must be the Hawks, just brought into the field by Summersailor. In numbers, I can see 20 divisions each of 2000 men. However, within the army of 40,000 men there appears to be a separate division of 2000 Hawks that are dressed differently. One hundred of the Hawk soldiers are now dispersed to each division.

"They are like a small teaspoonful of strong drink mixed in a gallon jug of clear spring water. Whoever drinks that jug will not get drunk. He'll never know that he has drunk hard liquor. It was foolish to water down the Hawks like that."

Then the scouts of the Hillwolves came back to camp and told the king and queen that they had seen enemies lurking and stalking in the hills above the camp.

Then War Queen Snakeknife took her makeup and the gear of a warriorwoman and gave them to a singing, servant girl and storyteller who was elegant and looked like a warrior queen. The girl was told to walk around the camp.

When Maplewine saw the girl dressed as a warrior queen, she threw a light javelin at her before Whaleroarer had a chance to intervene. The javelin transfixed the singer, and yet not one of the Hillwolves standing by seemed in the least concerned as she lay dying.

"It seems I have killed a harmless servant girl," said Maplewine. "I wish I had not been so thoughtless or so hotheaded. No doubt the dead one is no queen but only a singer."

Whaleroarer tried to calm down Maplewine, "No matter, no one is harmless among the enemy. Even a singer brings laughter and happiness and helps to build up courage in the foe."

***

Ratrunner had been told to note the place from where the hasty javelin had been thrown to kill the girl posing as Queen Snakeknife. Then Ratrunner threw out his fiery spear that shook out poisoned flames upon the Whaleroarer and on Maplewine, their charioteer and horses. However, the Seagulls' battle armor and shields protected them as they fled away to find a sheltered place.

Ratrunner hid himself among his rats and tortured them with fire, then stirred them up with sick and poisoned food.

Then King Warchariot sent three birds of message to tell his farout ranks that enemies were skulking in the hills and snowy woods.

Maplewine threw more javelins that transfixed two birds in mid-air and they never took their message to the far battle flanks but the third bird escaped and soon delivered its warwarning. But rumor soon began to filter through the ranks that armies of the Wavewarriors were invading.

It happened at this time that War Queen Snakeknife had sent out for storytellers and songwriters, friendly to the Wolves, to come to speak and sing and boost the Hillwolves' bravery. When these entertainers came to the Hillwolves' camp, they were set upon and slaughtered in mistake by the Hillwolves who had failed to recognize the storytellers and songwriters as friends. They mistakenly thought that those bards had been spies sent from the Wavewarriors to deceive them.

So it was that Whaleroarer and Maplewine hid in the snowy woods while the wolves jumped out at friends and shook the hands of demons.

CHAPTER FOUR
KILLERS IN WAITING

At this time, the great boat Waterfight came ashore among the rocky snowlands in the west coast of the peninsula of Warchariot and the Hillwolves. Stormleaper, with the help of Streamflower, was captain of the boat that was filled with all the fine accoutrements of war.

The moon rose on the camp of the Hillwolves that was now being stalked by the small company of Wavewarriors.

The black and yellow Mooncrow flew across the sky, reporting all it saw to the witches. The snow lay thick on all the trees around the camp as the Seagulls dug out a clear shelter.

Stormleaper made a bed then lay down low, the way an old cat goes to its rest at night. Head close to ground, twisting and turning around among the grass, he made a place for himself where he could curl up snugly and lie asleep. So the Stormleaper snugged himself in blankets and placed his weapons and accoutrements around him.

Then Warchariot sent out his magic killers led by a warrior blazing like a torch; a firefiend from the pit of endless flames, shaped like a human creature going to battle.

The firefiend's head was covered with a hundred jewels. His skin was crimson as it smoked and fumed. His eyes and mouth were filled with flames and sparks.

Each eye had seven pupils, burning brightly. Each hand had seven fingers and each foot had seven toes. His nails were long and sharp, as strong and fiercely gripping as a gorilla's nails.

His limbs and body also shot out flames as did his sword and spears and shoes and helmet and his shield blazed like the round mouth of the pit.

Slow and stumbling was his stilted stride as he loomed closer to the Seagull camp, waving his sword and yelling threats of firedeath, "I will burn to death all those whom I can touch."

Streamflower yelled, "Aim at the trees above him."

Then she and Stormleaper and their servants, all flung high their spears and javelins at the branches of the trees surrounding the dread man of fire. Surely and swiftly snow fell down upon him and all his flames were doused in the falls of winter. The man of fire burnt up and shriveled into a heap of ashes crumpling in the snow.

But hiding in the trees above the firefiend were three white forms of near-dead murderers. They had been waiting for a chance to kill the Seagull warriors if they had escaped the fire. Now they fell from the trees. Pierced by the Seagulls' spears, they screamed for mercy.

"Yes, we will be merciful, for we will kill you," Streamflower answered coldly.

And Stormleaper hacked them to pieces with his battle axe and cried, "I have no time to keep your heads. The wild dogs in the bushes roar and yelp."

Then Stormleaper seized a shovel and threw their pieces into the bushes where the wild dogs howled.

This was the fate of the disguised Wolves. For these dead ones were the stalkers and disguisers who were dressed in suits of white to creep and murder through the forest of snow. Those dread unseen assassins would suddenly appear upon their prey and stab them to death before the victims knew that cowardly assassination was upon them.

But other members of this Killer Clan with glue holding together their barkwood suits, were lurking in the fields and nearby forest.

The next morning at dawn as they left their camp, Stormleaper asked his Wavewarriors if they could see any disguisers.

Streamflower and their servants all shook their heads.

"We cannot see any of them," replied Streamflower, "either they are not there or they are well hidden. Let us move slowly and watch for leaping trees or grass or bushes."

Stormleaper shook his head, "They are too fast. Before we can see them, we will all be dead. We have been in danger ever since that Mooncrow observed us and reported back to the witches on our exact location."

Then Streamflower peered into the woods ahead and warned the servants, "Beware too of the wilddogs lurking ahead."

But Stormleaper shook his head in disagreement, "Beware nothing: those dogs did not eat us. Those are the dogs that ate our enemies."

Stormleaper lifted up two bits of meat leftover from the bodies of the disguisers and threw them far ahead into the tall trees that lined the way and also threw one out to the tall green grasses of the field. Soon the wilddogs had picked up the scents.

The Stormleaper and Streamflower and all their servants held up their slender javelins at the ready.

One set of cunningly disguised assassins were hidden deep among the trees, darkdressed in bark and saplings and in green-brown branches.

The other kill-group lurked among the grasses, dressed in green leaves and flowers and long rushes, just as the sun began to melt the snow.

The dogs smelt out the close clan of disguisers, their blood and bone and glue and grass and bark. The dogs growled, snarled and snapped and foamed at them. Then getting no response from the hiding killers lying in wait, the dogs threw themselves upon the clan and began to tear them apart and eat them.

As the killers broke from disguise, to save their lives, they drew their knives and javelins against the dogs. Once they had seen where the disguisers stood, Stormleaper and Streamflower let fly their thin darts and impaled the masqueraders of kill. The wild dogs dined on the bones of those assassins, then howled and lurked nearby, baying for more.

Slowly Stormleaper moved forward with Streamflower and their troop towards the camp of the Hillwolves.

The Mooncrow, resting by day in the great castle, could not spy now as she had done during the darkening night and so Warchariot consulted the four witches and was told, "Send out our deadliest killers to destroy them. For the Stormleaper and his javelin queen are drops of windblown rain before the coming storms and if not stopped, ten thousand storms will follow."

So King Warchariot sent out the three Deathhead dwarfs to attack the hill from where Stormleaper was watching the Hillwolf army. This was a slippery hillock of ice and snow and trees and bushes.

The three Deathhead dwarfs were carrying the iron flails and swinging them with their powerful apely hands, all wrinkled and knarled. From each flail there hung seven strong chains with seven iron apples on each chain and sharpspiked poisoned thorns on every ball. The dwarf Deathheads, strutting from side to side like mad gorillas, rushed on the Seagull camp as Stormleaper's spears bounced briskly off their bodies. Even their eyelids were as hard as stone. Swinging their flails they walked a deadly walk, laughing and foaming at the thought of killing. Their heads, each with four eyes, rolled and roamed, looking out for prey.

One of the Deathhead dwarfs slipped for a moment upon the ice. Swift as a silver javelin, Stormleaper flung himself upon the ice and slid downhill to seize the Deathhead's flail then cut the fallen Deathhead dwarf to pieces. He threw himself, and his newfound Deathhead flail, in fury upon the other two Deathhead dwarfs and with his greater height and reach, he soon destroyed them both.

First the iron apple with venom thorns cut into the dwarfs' mouths.

Their teeth and tongues were ripped out. The iron ball returned once more to smash the roof of the mouth. The white and bloody clot of brain was also ripped out with the apple, as blow on blow was flailed upon the dwarfs, by their own deadly weapon.

This ball cut them to mince so small that they might well have been passed through a cornmeal sieve. The Deathheads' flail sliced with sharp and frenzied butchery. Even the wild dogs could not eat their bodies but pawed and picked the pieces of their bones that lay around like pebbles on the shore. In this way, all three dwarfs were smashed to pieces.

Then the Mooncrow once again spied over the camp of Stormleaper and told the tale to War Queen Snakeknife.

"They are still alive. I just cannot believe it," cried Snakeknife, "send out our deadliest killers. Unleash the three friars from the pit of pestilence, led by

Ratrunner, Abbot of Black Death. Those friars cannot be killed. They are dead already. Even their rats are dead, unnatural creatures from the deep abyss of pain where death is spawned. The three black monks have sick and ulcered skin. These are the twisted friars, concocting germs, breeding foul deadly strains of fever and cancer and inculcating all these into sick rats to set upon their foes."

So the undead friars were sent out to destroy.

Stormleaper saw these bent and twisted ghouls rushing close upon his troop. These ghouls were led by the Ratrunner, Abbot of the Black Monks. Stormleaper transfixed all four with his spears.

The monks began to struggle, squirm and squeal and bleed in anguish as they struggled to remove the rough spears from their bodies. Even the

Ratrunner writhed in pain on the ground.

In their hot fever against the Stormleaper, they released their rats, pointing them toward Stormleaper and Streamflower.

But the rats sensed that their masters now were weak and, though not dying, were bleeding in agony. So the rats seized their revenge upon the friars who had injected them with vile diseases and tortured them with cancers to pass on. The rats, creatures of death and deadly sickness, opened their mouths and tore the monks apart.

They set about devouring the devious Ratrunner whose strange vials and smoking test tubes had long woven webs of infectious pain and feverish death.

The rats, the Ratrunner and the monks of death suffered the pains their victims long had suffered before they all descended into the pit of pestilence from which they had been called.

Back in the Castle of Warchariot and his War Queen Snakeknife, the Mooncrow told them of how Abbot Ratrunner and his monks and rats had all slipped back into the pit of pestilence in the ill universe.

Summersailor shook his head, "We may yet regret breaking up the great Hawkarmy. These Wavewarriors have destroyed our main assassins and yet their king, the Wallwave, has not acted nor even his second in command Icedragon has not yet raised a hand. They have just bought time for their fragmented fleet to mend together."

War Queen Snakeknife laughed loudly, "You have been fortunate to choose the winning side. Your great Hawkarmy are better fed and equipped than ever before. Think of the Wavewarriors, their King Wallwave is but a boy. We'll see how he measures up to a man's job, as he tries to win, even though he is outnumbered.

"As for Icedragon, he ran away in fear of all of us to join the young boy's army. Icedragon is mature. His white-blond hair is natural, in youth, but soon the first grayness comes as it has long since come to you Summersailor and after that who knows? He may remain a battlehardened warrior or he may crumble just like the snows of autumn. We will wait and see.

"Our Hillwolf Warriors outnumber the Seagulls of the world. As for our leading killers falling, as you have falsely imagined Summersailor, laugh and loudly laugh. I warn you while you may. Yes, laugh before you are taken for a fool.

"Our hidden powers of killing have scarcely yet been seen. We have the power to bring fear to the foe. The four witches can appear as ladies of great beauty although they are withered up and cruel and treacherous and toothless and warted and bald and poisonclawed. Everyman needs a witch and an angel near him. In this short life it is impossible for any living man to tell the difference.

"Spells of the witches also can change shapes of men and women to animals or birds so that our Hillwolves can go out to fight disguised as apes or dogs or boars or bears, striking great fear into the hearts of many. For fear is in the mind, not of reality. Fear is in the soul, and in the eyes, so do not think lightly of our shapeshifting. The thing you think you see can change your mind and turn you from hot courage to cold terror.

"We have a potion that will merge your memory into the mind of an ape for three long days and there you dwell at the intersection of two worlds, letting you kill your enemies with a gorilla's strength."

"I do not like it," Summersailor replied, "I would fear that I could not return or escape from the ape body."

Snakeknife answered, "So what? If you remained an ape you could control and rule the world with mind of man and body of a gorilla.

"Of course, there are other forms of shapeshifting and illusion such as protectors at your side who seem to be strange creatures from the pit, images from the demonic mirror of life."

Summersailor shook his head, "I will fight on as a man by my own hand and heart."

"Do so," Snakeknife replied, "But do remember this. The powers on our side are supernatural. See the old Mooncrow lurking at our windows. She is a flyer over the night and waters, a warrior witch of devious craft and cunning. Soon she will cripple and confuse the Seagulls. Summersailor, after you have gone to your room no doubt you wonder whether you have acted wisely in joining us. Be assured you have. There are two kinds of mighty spirit in the universe. There are the powers of good and powers of win: those who are good but losing and those who win."

"I must disagree with you Queen Snakeknife," replied the Summersailor, "as the commander of a mighty army, now broken up in fragments, I do brood at times but not to doubt myself. No, I worry about the fighting spirit of the Hawks now that they must fight without the help and skills of all their comrades, now they have lost the tricks of camaraderie of moving their fighting men and chariots and weapons from one part of the battlefield to another. And what has come to replace this comradeship? Nothing has replaced it.

"Also, we should be bringing out the singers of songs, composers and musicians. Storytellers would uplift the

Hawks and dancers would make the warriors feel tall and strong. There is more to war than killing and knife-cunning, more than mere butchery and ruthlessness. Their hearts and minds must be raised, not just their spears."

Snakeknife replied, "Your Hawks are fed and wined. I would not grieve for them, they are well cared for. Your army is sure to win – that is all they need."

CHAPTER FIVE
COMBATS OF KILL

When King Wallwave landed his longboat in the east, he met with the Icedragon who was coming from the west of the bowlshaped peninsula of the Hillwolves.

At once the two agreed on their battle plans as they surveyed the peninsula from their chariots late in the night, watched by the black Mooncrow.

As they made their plans, the Wallwave pointed out, "The armies of the Hillwolves are too great for our Seagulls to attack them, head on head. Their fighting men would be too many for us now that we have lost our crack division with Summersailor and his skills of war. He is our kinsman and we much regret that he has left us. Perhaps he will come back and fight on our side once more, like you Icedragon. So let us quietly build up our fleet while we engage some of their heroes in single combat."

"Yes," Icedragon agreed, "That is the best plan, single combat. Soon the spring will come again and we need to give more time to Summersailor to think about his place with Warchariot. That is why we should not send out any boats or our main fleet until the spring has come. Then we can launch our farflung friends and ships. At this dark time of year the winds are fierce. The pathways are snow-laden and each gap is a tunnel of cold wind where rivers are flooding.

"Yet the winter is far spent, soon spring will come; so wait for the spring and warmth before we sail. Then the fords, in the mellowing springtime of the year, will be shallow and can be easily driven through. The paths will be clear and dry and marchable. Then the thick green leaves on the bushes will become shelters and covers for our advancing men. Greenswards will act as pillows for our nighttime army. Young stallions will be stronger, then nights will be shorter and it is easier to keep watch for the enemy.

"Our plan of single combat will help us to hold back the tide of war. In single combat each side can lose only a single warrior at one time. If they decline to duel, they will be seen as cowards by their own warriors who will refuse to follow them into battle.

"Meanwhile our fleet can be built up with the repair and rigging of ships and chariots. We can smarten up in general training, in skills, in arms and in men."

Then the two great warriors sped their chariots forward and waved their swords at the Mooncrow in the sky.

Icedragon shook his spear and called for combat as the black spy flapped her wings and screeched in hatred. Then the Mooncrow flew up high and drove the clouds away from the face of the moon and the light shone on a huge band of Hillwolves lying in wait, just ahead, where there was light enough to fight.

The Icedragon challenged them, "I will accept you but only as one warrior at a time. I will fight against you all in single combat. Now is your chance to kill me, so seize your weapons."

Then the Icedragon whipped his chariot upon them. It was a quick and effective onslaught. He steered his horses towards them, fiercely flinging his sharp and terrifying spears and javelins, hammered and molded from iron and tense steel, beaten with a strong arm in the fires of triumph.

Great was the pomp and pride of his brave horses as their tails and manes shook out and shone and tossed.

A hero light glowed all around Icedragon, a halo of fire and brightness flashed about him as he called out his deadly oath of combat, "A battle is not a battle unless a hero has been death slaughtered or brought low in homage. I swear that I will slay great warriors or else I will myself be slaughtered here."

Then the Icedragon took to slash and hack, and arms and legs and heads fell round about like the green boughs of pears and apples and plums, in the autumn of a red and yellow orchard, as the Hillwolves and their horses fled away.

Likewise, Wallwave gave out his battle challenge to the fleeing foe to bring them back to battle, "I do expect your bravest and your best. So let a high spirit and courage rise up in you, for what you do today will be long retold. Each one of you will be marked for what he does. The tale of each one's work this battleday will be recorded in the annals of war forever.

"Also, it will be remembered what you said, and how you boasted, in your nights of wine. So remember now your wineboasts and your pledges.

"Announce for me a single combat challenger. I will fight, one to one, with any warrior now or at any time that meets your courage. I will rise up, wherever you may stand, like a cock crowing suddenly in the cold dawn. I will flap my wings like a bird and go to combat with the heavy harness of battle across my shoulders."

But still the Hillwolves ran away and skulked behind the trees and bushes and rocks of the forest. So the Wallwave with warrior friends and Whitehair standing beside him took to his great longboat to scour the coastlands and flush out the foe.

His yellow skin glowed like the rising sun in its hazy mesh of red and blue. He was an oriental prince of power and speed. He held the magic Bonespear in his hand.

He steered his ship along the withering sea, hard cutting, throwing aside the waves like waste. The wind knifed keen into Wallwave's face, attacking the son of Waterbear. It was like a charioteer spinning along an open road, with spears and swords and killer sythewheels slashing forward. So the boat flew, ringed around with swords and spears. In the prow of the boat stood the Wallwave, like the rising sun.

A cold wind blew across those dangerous blades of weapons, set up and pointed by a gang of howling ghosts. Lean phantoms shimmered in a solemn imitation of servingmen all grinning and offering to serve up drinks. Long knives and daggers and sharp forks and spoons lay on the silver plates. Places were set by the bowing, scraping, obsequious spirit servants.

The specters invited all, My good lords, drink, they shimmered and grinned and beckoned, offering to deal the drinks of death to all the Hillwolves.

When the Hillwolves refused these invitations, the Wallwave cried out to the Whaleroarer and to the Icedragon and the Stormleaper, "Let us now fight only against their leaders, for when the main boughs of the tree are severed, it will not take very long for the tree itself to be cut down. Likewise when a general falls, soon after will his people fall down also. Yet who will meet my challenge to combat me?"

Then Winterwarrior, fieldmarshal of the Hillwolves, standing ashore among his chariots, heard the great combat challenge of the Wallwave. As his grim warriors looked at him in silence, he called out to the Wallwave,

"Come ashore and I will gladly meet you to unseat you."

And Winterwarrior, veteran of many combats, a sly old wolf, bowed low in courtesy. A herolight shone all about the fieldmarshal, a halo of fire and brightness flashed around him. He was a hero with a heart of stone. His blue eyes were a glitter of ice, a burning glow of red coals, anger and blood. He was a keen warsurgeon of cold cutting scalpels, a chariotfighter, strong as a bull in fury.

Winterwarrior called to the men who followed him, "This story will be sung even among shepherds, wherever tales of war are told and retold."

Winterwarrior wore a cloak of crimson lambswool. His brow was like snow with cheeks of foxglove red. His eyebrows were black as beetles and his eyes were blue as sky. His fair hair curled and fell like a thick ram's mane till it sat upon his shoulder. He swung a sword of steel with a gold hilt. His shield of red was studded with gold and silver. In his left hand he shook a three-pronged spear.

Then the Wallwave steered his boat ashore and his men set up his chariot and arms and laid out his accoutrements of war, as the Wallwave held his magic Bonespear. He had carved out paths of blood and bones so many times in the ranks of the enemy like a keen and proud builder of green roads through jungle grasses, when he had trained to be a sea prince with Shadowhero.

Now he was a skilled warrior like the flames that spark and shoot and flicker through a palace roof in the dead of winter weather: a warrior like the spout of a hotwell that shoots into the air upward and splashing higher and higher: spurting hot for ever, a warrior like the mighty flow of water that pours out of the rock. A waterfall that pounds and foams and hazes into a mist down into the depths of a stream unending, as it stirs up from the seacellars of the deep. He was a true wallwave, flinging himself on earth, in a solid wall of fierce, unbeaten onslaught.

Winterwarrior again cried to the Wallwave, "I will accept your challenge to destroy you."

The fieldmarshal's chariot was driven out to meet the chariot of the true Wallwave.

Winterwarrior then ordered two henchmen to wait on either side, ahead of him, to close in on the Wallwave, unawares, and stab through the Wallwave from behind as he and the Winterwarrior battled together.

Then Wallwave flew upon the fieldmarshal like a great wave of the ocean on a toy, flung the Bonespear and then caught the Bonespear ahead as it flew on through Winterwarrior's throat. Never did the Wallwave slow nor even stop his speed but galloped over the Hillwolf's chariot, crushing to death the Winterwarrior and smashing to pieces his accoutrements.

The assassins lurking behind the wild Wallwave were left standing and stunned and at a loss.

The Wallwave kept control of his chariot as it flew over the bones of the Winterwarrior and pounded straight ahead into the battle. Wallwave rolled ahead and slashed and hacked. The ground shook over more than 1000 acres as the Wallwave carved a path fit for a king. Like a swift earthquake rattling over the fields, the tall, noble, elegant and warlike horses pulled the warchariot thundering over the land.

Yet these great stallions of the combat zone were lean and nimble and keen and breathing fire, cutting across great lumps of hills and through high waters over the fords of fighting streams and rivers.

Spears of the deadly thousands of the Hillwolves erectly stood high up in the chariots, gleaming and fiercely glinting in the sunlight; a threat to all but those in the chariot. Across the seated legs of warriors there sat the swords waiting to be seized and wielded. Silver shields hung on elbows ready for use. Helmets of burnished brasses crowned the heads.

Each horse was quick and easy to mount and steer with a strong bridle of twisted ropes and cords. In between the chariots roamed herds of extra horses, ready to be dragooned for the need of battle, steeds with large open nostrils and sharp eyes set in small heads. These steeds ran on broad hoofs and were easily caught and stopped. They were swift and dexterous for a sudden raid.

For when the Wallwave flattened a road of red that was fiery and tempestuous and true as steel, he carnaged to take revenge for the killing of his father, Waterbear.

There was an aura of revengekill around him like the smell of a deadly wild boar when it strikes. When a hero even looked on this solemn soldier, the hero's heart grew weak and his arms tingled with dread.

The Hillwolves faces grew black with fear and some warriors lost their strength. Some even lost their minds just to approach Wallwave.

Men, driven mad with fear, ran far away from him, screaming like ghosts.

The Wallwave sped through coolly and carved a path of broken bones from warriors and horses' bodies, straight as a roadway through a busy forest, like a pathway chopped out by an explorer's axe, through a red jungle, a place for men to walk, littered by chariot pieces and red bones. A rout fell out before him.

Some of the Hillwolves killed each other just to escape the Wallwave's sword of battle, just to avoid the scythe of death, the gravedigger's inexorable destruction.

The Wallwave's chariot advanced, leaving a wake of white and red dead bodies on the road just like the wake of foam behind his longboat.

CHAPTER SIX
DARK DESTINIES

After this great rout of the enemy, Wallwave made evening camp in the remote forest for all his warriors so that they could rest and eat and sleep.

Suddenly, a woman in black drove past in her chariot. The chariot was of burnt cinderwood as though both woman and chariot had been through a fire. The horses drawing her chariot were death black. Red cinders lined the chariot. She held two black shields and two swords of glittering black. Her skin and eyes were darker than the night. Three pupils moved around in both her eyes. The flowing robes she wore were of black silk.

The Shield of Roar cried out a call of warning that something dangerous had come into their camp.

Stopping her chariot in front of the Seagulls, she stared at the Wallwave for a long time. Then she drove away and looked ahead as she disappeared into the shadows and the shades of forest.

Then War Queen Whitehair told the Wallwave, "Bad things come. The look of that dark woman was long and deep and sorrowful. It frightens me. It is the harbinger of devildays ahead. Potions and spells are in the air. Crows will be satiated with the dead bones of men. Ravens will eat. Slaughter will scream. Blades will whip. Shields and mail will lie broken on the ground and in small pieces."

Wallwave told her sadly, "That is War. We did not start it. Soon it will be finished."

But Whitehair was still unsettled and spoke again to the Wallwave, "I can see mindmadness and insane delusion. I can see thought manipulation ahead and strange illusions driving the mind to dreams."

Wallwave answered thoughtfully, "Yes, I do see. I feel as though her eyes burned into my brain and stole a part of me, yet I remain whole and undivided."

Then Wallwave closed his eyes and bowed his head.

***

At that very moment, a sameshape of the Wallwave appeared before his younger brother, Stormbolt, who was far away in his snowy training camp.

Then this sameshape beckoned to young Stormbolt to join it in the chariot, a black and burnished chariot like that of the dark woman who had earlier stopped and stared at Wallwave.

The young Stormbolt had finished his day's practice, so he was dressed in tough mail, helmet and full armor of sword and dirks and spears and javelins, wearing his shield and all the accoutrements of battle.

Stormbolt entered the chariot and it fled away into the snowy and the silvery fields.

The old man, Shadowhero, who had been instructing Stormbolt, ran outside and chased after the dark burnt chariot, shouting, "Stormbolt beware. Was that really your brother or just an image of his counterpart from the pit?"

Then he paused and wept and shook his head, "But I am too old and cold to follow you. Perhaps one of our younger men should go to see if Stormbolt is being taken astray. Lured on to shades of sorrow in handcuffs of delusion to be walked down a path that leads to death. I smell a pungent odor of burning embers."

He turned aside and shook in fear, but others came to comfort him, "It was Wallwave. We all identified him. Even now you might hear his voice in the chariot. It was no sameshape mirage and no fetch."

Soon the two horses and the two ghostly forms in the phantom chariot were silenced in the mists of swirling, flying snow.

***

The sameshape of Wallwave had taken Stormbolt in the phantom chariot to the land of Warchariot and his War Queen Snakeknife.

Suddenly a voice, like the voice of Wallwave, spoke to Stormbolt, "Your uncle Summersailor has joined the foe."

The young Stormbolt was puzzled, "I did not know. My uncle did not tell me. What can I do?"

***

Awaiting the light of dawn and combat time in the dark silent camp of the Wallwave, the Whaleroarer asked for someone to look ahead and read to him the cards of fate and fortune from a cardpick of a set of cards.

So Maplewine shuffled the Deck of Destiny and Whaleroarer closed his eyes and chose five cards.

Maplewine told the warrior, whom she hoped to marry one day in the happy future, "Do not go out to fight for I can see that there is no good luck for you in this combat."

The deal of destiny from the cards was just a thought, a possibility of death, but a torment of the heart for Maplewine and a deathdanger for the Whaleroarer.

A loss of eyesight and a brief blackout, a dimness of the mind for just a moment, struck hard at Maplewine but she spoke on. "For you may not return alive and well."

But Whaleroarer replied, shaking his head, "I have never in all my life refused to go to any combat just because a seer foretold of bad luck coming or ill fate. It is my turn. I will match any Hillwolf, shoulder to shoulder and go step by step, sword drawn and pointed towards the enemy."

Then Maplewine answered him, "Please, Whaleroarer, do try at least to catch them unawares. If you can find a place to land a boat where they will least expect you. I can see fierce waves. I hear harsh words of harder men, arrogantly talking of your death, Whaleroarer, with barbarous and merciless derision. I hear dim voices whispering under bushes. Try to go slowly and tread tenderly."

Maplewine went in sorrow to her bed and cried all night. She did not sleep because of the bad omens.

Whaleroarer quietly took his supply of arms in darkness to his great boat but it was not his destiny to fall upon the foe in sudden victory.

That night it was the turn of the old wolf Cragfox to meet Whaleroarer in the field.

Cragfox determined not to fall unawares and had placed watchmen at every shore of landing to spy for any incursion of Seagulls in the peninsula where any ship might harbor.

Sadly, the Whaleroarer sailed to one such place and the wolfspies reported to Cragfox that the longboat of a Seagull was coming ashore. "See, the Whaleroarer's chariot is being hauled and set up with its horses and its accoutrements on the silver strand ready to take advantage of any Hillwolf in sudden single combat."

Cragfox was a cunning and sharp warrior. He rode to meet Whaleroarer at the cove where the Seagull was landing.

Chariots rushed to smash and clash against each other and Cragfox cast at the luckless Seagull, a mighty spear that tore the brave Whaleroarer's chest apart.

Whaleroarer did not accept this as a gift and mightily repaid the deadly favor with a strong javelin, thrown back in return, that ripped open the Cragfox and broke his back.

Both warriors now were wounded to the point where Death sent a strong whiff of the deathsmell lingering in the air above them and over them.

Although wounded to death they still fought on as an aura of the inevitable came down. Before they died a great fear came upon them, like the fear that brings stampede to many horses when they hear thunder and see the flash of lightning. And the fear of the Mooncrow flying overhead and screeching in circles gripped as both men fought, as a fear of the darkness closed out their minds.

The two men waged a hard and bitter last stand until their shields were shattered into pieces and then, without defenses, they struck each other.

So there began the harvest of the Mooncrow, the hacking and stabbing, wounding and dismembering. With hand and legs slashed off, until they fell together in the field, cut hand to hand, each heart beside pierced heart, legs beside legs, face to face, foot to foot in tandem stride with severed head lying beside hacked head.

And so the two men died at the same time, like twins who died together in cold age. They were two hardfought warriors who never were defeated by any living foe.

The dead killed by the dead.

CHAPTER SEVEN
STORMBOLT AND WITCHCRAFT

Maplewine mourned as she set up and purified the ship of Whaleroarer to prepare the bark for a hero's funeral to the Isles of Youth.

***

At the first splash and trickle of the spring, the Seagulls began to rustle in their nests, the trees put on their spotted greenbud tunics and snows drained away and ice began to melt. The small skiffs and the longboats of the Seagull Warriors edged out to sea, to invade the land of the Hillwolves.

Wallwave sailed his longboat over the waves, unshipped his weapons once again and drove his wild horses of war through the Hillwolves, slaughtering many like a wild tornado.

His chariot ploughed through the army of the foe, like his great ship cutting up the waves of the sea, leaving behind a foaming redwake of bones, flying and lying in the green field of battle. Heads, skulls, entrails, arms, legs scattered around like a cold crop of hailstones or like stormrocks that had fallen from a mountain in a growling earthquake.

***

As one Hillwolf lay dying, he cried out, "Let me die out at sea where I have lived among the seals and dolphins and the seaweed. Let me die with the smell of seasalt in my nostrils. Take me out there I beg of you, Wallwave."

So Wallwave threw the bleeding man, in full view of the battle, across his shoulders, carried him to the sea and swam him out to where the Icedragon's boat lay near the shore. Then the Wallwave swam back to join the battle.

So the Icedragon's men saw how the Wallwave had brought the weak man out beside their boat and thought the dying man had been one of theirs who had been wounded in the battle ashore. The wounded man swam close to Icedragon's boat and asked the Seagulls to help him come aboard.

One of Icedragon's men stretched out his hand to pull the Hillwolf into the great boat but the Hillwolf, even as he was dying, seized hard upon the wrist of the Wavewarrior, pulled him into the sea with a sharp grip and drowned him with great force.

As the dying Hillwolf drowned the Wavewarrior, he cried out to all the Seagulls and the Hillwolves, "Death to all Wavewarriors. Even with my last faint gasp of breath I hold down a Wavewarrior and drown him."

And neither the Wolf nor the Seagull were ever seen again for the Hillwolf clung to the Seagull like the bite of a mad pitbull, through all their drowning struggles.

And all who stood ashore in the battle heard the boast of the dying Hillwolf as he drowned his foe. Many in the ranks of the Hawkarmy who were divided up among the Hillwolf's forces were watching. They saw what had happened and with what treachery and deceit the Seagull, their former friend and fellow Wavewarrior, had been murdered by the Wolf.

They noted this and stored it in their memories, but for now they mostly stayed in place for the sake of loyalty and also out of fear of the Summersailor who now fighting their former friends the Wavewarriors in the field of brutal and unforgiving battle.

Some of the Hawkarmy secretly rebelled and mutinied and set fire to the Wolves' buildings, as they burnt both serf and noble, women and children, setting aflame both dog and man. They scorched to cinders both drinking horns and silver cups and plates. They burnt chairs, bowls and tables and woolen carpets and tapestries and trophies of old wars, all under cover of the raging battles.

Some of the Wolves, suspecting this sly sabotage, secretly stabbed one or two Hawkwarriors. A swift knife in the back dispatched the suspects but so the Wolves lost those Hawks' help in battle.

So the Wolves paid a pretty and a princely price for the treachery that cost the life of one Seagull.

***

Some of the warriors of Warchariot refused to fight for him and hid away in hills and caves and in remote stone islands, because of the cruel taxes that Warchariot had fixed upon them.

As they told the envoy of the Wallwave, "We will help you win with food and fish and weapons, while we have them, for none of us would dare eat a deer or trout or even a bird brought down by any hawk, for fear of being taxed for it by King Warchariot. None of us would dare marry off a daughter for fear of being asked if she is betrothed to any of the men of Warchariot. If she is not then she must pay a tax to the Snakeknife. No farmer dares to grow a crop unless he pays a tax to King Warchariot. These brutal taxes are supposed to be for bringing protection to us in time of war, yet here is war and we are taxed and fined and also asked to help fight for the king, a double curse."

***

Then the Seagull fleet continued sailing through the soft icecaps to join with the Wallwave, who marshaled all their boats and directed them, as more Wavewarriors joined the fleet of war. Wallwave sent them through the green seamountains and the seals lay back and watched and the swordfish cut through the seaweed like the scythes of chariots slicing through corn on a late autumn day.

Wallwave sent out secret envoys at nighttime to encourage some of the Hawk brigades to return to fight once more for the Wallwave but they feared to take an open stand against the Summersailor.

Still, Wallwave marshaled his new fleet and laid out plans for the attacks on the Hillwolves.

***

Meanwhile, at the castle of King Warchariot and War Queen Snakeknife, the younger brother of Wallwave, Stormbolt, was being harnessed and prepared for single battle with his uncle Summersailor.

Warchariot, Queen Snakeknife and the four Witches of Kill were conspiring with magic potions to suppress old memories in the mind of Stormbolt.

They gave Stormbolt a new name, the warname of Strangelook and told him it was best for him not to know his true identity in the coming combats so that old friends who had changed sides would not misclaim his loyalty or his sympathy.

"You have not been here before, Strangelook, so you cannot know who is friend or foe but we will tell you."

Then Queen Snakeknife took King Warchariot aside and asked, "Why do we not just stab or poison him now that we have young Stormbolt in our power?"

But Warchariot replied, "Now is a time for war and changing loyalties. When Summersailor defeats young Stormbolt it will be devastating to the Wallwave and all his Seagulls when his younger brother is killed by our main champion and hero. Because of this great victory, Summersailor will bolster his authority over our Hawks.

"Now that we have lost all the masqueraders, the man of fire, the three Deathhead dwarfs as well as Winterwarrior, Oakhill, Cragfox, the Ratrunner and the Flying Bat, all our best men lost at the hands of the Seagulls by mere mischance, we need the Summersailor to have a great victory to bring together our uneasy factions."

King Warchariot continued, "The Hawks, our crack division, and those who envy them: those who still hate to pay their taxes: all must then respect a veteran such as Summersailor."

Snakeknife replied, "Summersailor is indeed a hero. A herolight shimmers all around his head. A halo of fire and brightness flashes around him and we do need him now that war is furious but yet the Summersailor is past his best and Stormbolt is a young man, having just about completed his war training, keen and balanced.

"A younger hero must have a chance of winning in any duel that is hard fought against a veteran. Let us unleash the four sly shapeshifters, the witches of many spells and many forms: the Windweasel, Rivershark, Landslink and Meteoreyes as a baldeagle, a shark, a treesnake and a maddog to attack Stormbolt and to defend Summersailor."

"Do so," replied Warchariot, "but remember; tell the four witches to remain down low and not to be seen much. Keep their cunning help a secret stab for victory or we will be blamed for ganging up on young Stormbolt and murdering him. We need to enjoy the glory of our victories."

***

Now, at this time, in the spellroom of the Mooncrow, young Stormbolt was being armed for combatfight. The Hillwolf servants helped set up his accoutrements with hardmail tunic and high boots of steel. They fitted a close helmet with a slat for eyesight over a woolen knitted face and head mask, so that even his kinsmen would not know him.

The Mooncrow was there with the four witches, weaving their visions at the web of falsehood. The witches wore their shapes of dazzling beauty, dressed in fair flowing robes of loveliness to the eyes of men but not to the eyes of women.

The witches took a mist from the far sea, conjured up from the islands of the east and mixed it with a herb of forgetfulness. They gave it to Stormbolt to smell and drink so that his mind was not clear in its memories and they reminded him that his warname was Strangelook.

Suddenly a figure appeared at the barred castle window. It was an old poor man bent over and stiff with age. His clothes were worn and baggy and threadbare. His head was bald above his wrinkled face. Feeble and shaky, aching in limbs and joints, his legs supported by a walking stick that he leaned on. He crept up to the window and croaked at Stormbolt, "Let me talk to you."

"Go away," cried the four witches, pointing their long fingers.

"What do you say, Youngman?" asked the old one.

"Come in and welcome," replied Stormbolt.

The witches flung themselves on the door and locked it, screaming out curses on the old man's head as he disappeared at the barred window.

Then Landslink muttered in fear to the other witches, "The Truthteller is an old man and poor of clothing. Keep him outside or our champion will see clearly."

Then Truthteller stepped through the castle wall and groaned as he stretched his back and bent his knees, "Oh dear, you make me work in my old age." He moaned at the witches and shook his stick at them. They cringed in terror and hid their eyes away from the light of truth flashing out from his stick.

The form of loveliness fell from off their shoulders, like a cloak of flowers and blooms on an autumn day, and they were seen by all for what they were. They now appeared as the four Witches of Kill with warted fingerclaws filled with fatal venom and dressed in the rags of sick old age and neardeath.

The four witches, when they saw that they stood revealed, fled into the shadows screaming against Truthteller.

Then the old man in poor clothing spoke to young Stormbolt, "I am the Truthteller. I must warn you. Beware of manipulation and beware of mindmadness and beware of false voices that misguide. You are a sudden bolt shot from a storm, a bolt of lightning shot out one time only. You will fight one fight and then be celebrated forever and a day. . ."

Stormbolt replied, "If I could have only one day of glory, renown and honor, that is all that I would ever ask. I would be satisfied."

"That is well said," responded the Truthteller solemnly. "One great battle is all you will ever win. Promise me that your great combat will be all that you fight or all you seek to fight. Promise me that you will fight only one time."

Stormbolt promised, "I will fight only once."

The old man in poor clothing bowed to Stormbolt in a recognition of this solemn promise. Then he gave the youth a pebble on a string with a fishhook attached. "Take this fishhook and keep it by you on your battle belt.

You will need it to defeat your many foes."

Stormbolt put the fishhook in his belt with care, "I am not going fishing but I thank you, Truthteller, for your help."

When Stormbolt looked up again the old man in poor clothing had disappeared.

CHAPTER EIGHT
STRANGELOOK

In the shadows of the castle, the four witches of kill: the Windweasel, the Rivershark, the Meteoreyes and the Landslink transformed themselves into wild animals to attack Stormbolt and to distract him while he fought in single combat with Summersailor.

Windweasel took the form of a bald eagle; Rivershark took the form of a blood hungry shark; Meteoreyes took the shape of a maddog foaming and frothing at the teeth with deadly bite and Landslink took the form of a treesnake that hid and crawled with an envenomed spit.

Then the two heroes, Stormbolt and the Summersailor were escorted forward, each with his henchmen, to the place of combat, a clearing in the woods near to the castle. Many of the warriors of both Hillwolves and the Seagulls laid down their arms to watch the single combat.

The witches in their deadly animal forms were slinking and creeping along the branches, weeds and bushes as they hid in the riverbed of the forest.

Warchariot and his War Queen Snakeknife watched the combat from the battlements.

The witch Landslink, who was now in the form of a treesnake, raised her head out of her lair deep in the foliage. Stormbolt, throwing his chisel-pointed dagger, cut her head off. Then, with his swinging fishhook, he picked up the snakehead and threw it at the shark that jumped out of the water to devour him. The shark was choking on the venomed treesnake's bile as it fell back into the river coughing and choking.

The circling eagle swooped down upon young Stormbolt who swung his fishhook and ripped out its throat.

The half-dead eagle then flew at the Summersailor and blinded him as bloody specks and feathers fluttered in his face, distracting him and turning him inadvertently from the fight. Summersailor beat away the specks of blood and all the dust of fluttering feathers from his mail helmet and his blurring eyes.

The maddog lurched at Stormbolt who stood back and seized an old hollow log that had been left by the Truthteller for Stormbolt's protection. Stormbolt rammed the log into the mouth of the maddog, who bit upon it strongly, sinking its teeth into the mossy wood so that the log stuck in the maddog's mouth. Stormbolt swung his fishhook on the pebble into the hollow log with a great power so that it entered down the maddog's throat. The fishhook caught itself on the dog's heart and Stormbolt ripped it out with a sharp pull so that the dog rolled over and lay dead.

Then the four spirits of the witches flew back to the shades and spells of their dark castle, leaving the bodies of the savage killers: the shark, the tree-snake, the maddog and the eagle all lying dead before the young Stormbolt.

Warchariot and his War Queen Snakeknife stood up and yelled.

King Warchariot cried out, "Either Strangelook is very lucky or there is some kind of magic working on his side. In either case we need to dread this day."

And a deadly silence fell upon the watching hosts, for luck was on the side of the Stormbolt. Younger and swifter than the Summersailor, Stormbolt leapt high and flung his javelin straight through the throat and spine of Summersailor who staggered, slightly blinded by the dead eagle that the powers of win had tried to use to help him.

A smooth rainbow swung across the sky as Summersailor threw away his sword into the red wind of that final battle, knowing that the day of swords was gone. Then a mighty roar rang out in the forest glade as Summersailor seized the javelin that had transfixed his throat from front to back. Summersailor tried to pull the weapon out, then sighed and lay back in a pool of blood.

As Stormbolt cut off the head of Summersailor, War Queen Snakeknife seized the arm of Warchariot, "What can we do now? We are well defeated. We have lost our hero, Summersailor."

"We have lost other heroes in the past," responded Warchariot, "We still survive."

War Queen Snakeknife thought about their plight and then cried out,

"Perhaps this is not all bad. Strangelook is under our control and spells. Now we must hail him as our new leading champion. Most of our warriors will follow him and we will win the war against Wallwave.

"Later, the Wallwave must fight with his own brother and this can only work out well for us, for now the Wallwave cannot win. No matter what the outcome may yet be, Wallwave loses. Even if he wins, he loses deep in his mind. For who could remain sane after he has slain his younger and not yet experienced brother. See there, Stormbolt, even now he is a child."

Now that Stormbolt had killed their champion Summersailor, the witches, Warchariot and his War Queen Snakeknife changed their battlecries. They praised Stormbolt, now known as Strangelook, as their new champion.

"Hail to Strangelook who beheaded Summersailor. Old Summersailor was always a true Seagull at heart and all along planned to destroy us, cunningly and with deception, from within. So do not touch the body of Summersailor but let it lie there on the stiff field of battle as a witness that he was not one of us. Let us defeat the Seagulls first and then we can drive out the Hawkarmy as well."

So the two keen and eager armies threw themselves upon each other.

The Hillwolf army were urged by the four witches, the king and queen, to follow behind Stormbolt, now known as Strangelook. They shouted for the armies to close ranks behind their champion Strangelook their victorious hero and forcing him on to meet the Seagulls led by the Wallwave.

Stormbolt, mindful of his promise to Truthteller not to fight a second combat, held himself back but cheers of victory and praises for his fighting, strong pats of joy and friendship on his back, swept the young Stormbolt forward to the foe.

The force of his supporters jostled and mobbed and crowded the young prince forward in the battle to meet the great Wallwave, his elder brother, in mortal combat.

Both the grim armies flew upon each other like great forests of dense trees, with high boughs interlocking, fiercely and angrily slashing at each other. The cracking sounds of swords cutting off bones, hacking off arms, feet, legs and spines and heads. These sounds re-echoed with the roar of waves pounding upon the shore. Scrunching was heard of crushed bones, screaming out of mangled bodies, black eyesight of pierced eyes. Deafness of cut earsockets, with ears falling upon the ground like autumn leaves drifting. Fingers and toes, cold and hurting, through lying on the ground, severed from their late owner.

Mothers and fathers screamed for their dead young ones, lost in carnage. Wives wailed for husbands who had run away with the other woman Death and who would never return to their own homes.

Howlings of fear screeched out from the black spirits of the Mooncrow. The Shield of Roar cried out in agony, foretelling of more destruction on the way.

The blattering of the waves against the shore: the winds of ship destruction and drowning men: the rains that attack houses and submerge them: all joined in the wild screaming: "We will kill."

Grey tombstones leapt out of the holy ground and threw themselves upon the two great armies, to aggravate and infuriate both sides, driving each army to terrorize the other.

Trees that had stood for centuries, calm and helpful to mankind, giving fruit of apples, pears, plums, orange and mulberries, uprooted themselves and beat upon the warriors of both sides. Both Seagulls and Hillwolves were driven to frenzies of killing and maiming without mercy or conscience.

Even the greenhills set themselves on fire, regurgitating the bodies of the long dead, flying among the living, causing fear and horrible trembling as they prophesied, "You will die and for your murders go to the pit from which there is no escape for eternity. You will all die of agony and torture."

And the spirits of the dead laughed and toothgrinned and pointed their fingers at the living, crying, "YOU. You will be soon dead like us, come join us."

And when the living warriors wept, "No, No," the red demons of death cried, "Kill then Kill."

The Mooncrow and her ravens flew around and flapped through the thin wisps of cloud and urged them on to kill each other. Then strange women, spirits of hatred in the low caves of earth, dwelling in soil and darkness, wept and wailed and joined in laughing out, "Then kill, kill, kill." And all the specters of slaughter pointed fingers and yelled, "Kill, maim and chop or we will kill you. Kill."

And the warriors on each side, afraid of death, fell to the killing of the enemy and showed no mercy as they maimed and chopped and butchered in a bloodfast chilled insanity.

Then the bodies lay so thick upon the greenery that there was not as much as a blade of grass or a handful of brown earth to be seen around between the bodies of the dead war heroes.

When Wallwave saw the mayhems and the savagery of the two armies, he asked, "Who is that fighting warrior leading the Hillwolves, killing all those before him like a scythe on the wheels of a chariot in the fire of battle?"

Then the Wallwave was told by the grapevine of the battles, "That is Strangelook the new champion of the Hillwolves. He has slaughtered your uncle Summersailor who went over to join the foe."

Then Wallwave pondered this odd turn of events. "This is strange indeed. It may be that Summersailor had planned to bring his crack division back home to fight with us once more against the Hillwolves. Why would the Hillwolves war with Summersailor?"

"We do not know," Wallwave was told.

The Wallwave answered, "I must kill Strangelook, for only that can turn the tide of battle back in our favor now that we are outnumbered."

Some of the tax rebels and some Hawks now fought against their former allies the Hillwolves so that Warchariot was ringed around with foes.

Then the Wallwave pointed his charioteer towards Stormbolt and swung his great axe high and balanced the Bonespear high upon his shoulder. The Bonespear quivered and hummed for a hero's blood. Wallwave poured himself out upon the field like a noble river over rocks and stones, burning and crumbling everything before it or like a seawave pounding upon a bonewhite strand.

And the Hillwolves fled before him, like small children running away from a great wave of the ocean. For the Wallwave was the wallwave of all wallwaves, like a huge forest fire roaring and flaming and eating all before it, over the hills thick and intense and choking off all life.

***

Then the two brothers stood before each other. Stormbolt, who was now known as Strangelook saw the weapons of Wallwave and recognized them. He remembered them as weapons from a dream or sleeping vision, from where or when he did not know. But he knew that they were the weapons that would destroy him. He flung his spear at the Wallwave but the throw was cold without a flash or flame.

The Bonespear needed only a brief flick from the fingers of the Wallwave and it leapt to keep its foretold destiny and its thirst for hero blood, deep in the throat of Strangelook.

Then the Wallwave looked evenly at his brother. He stabbed Strangelook through the heart with his broadsword and seized the Bonespear out of the neck and spine of Strangelook and took his axe and struck his brother's head off. As the head rolled away it moaned, "These are the weapons of my elder brother. So let me be remembered for the one fight that surely turned the tide of war."

Then Stormbolt died.

The many warriors who stood close by heard Strangelook's words and pondered them.

Wallwave did not understand but took the face mask and the helmet from the head of Strangelook who was really his younger brother Stormbolt.

Then he saw what he had done and screamed aloud and wept.

The word went out to all that the Wallwave had been tricked into beheading his younger brother.

Then all the warriors standing nearby backed away and whether they were friend or enemy, they all fled for their lives.

CHAPTER NINE
KILLFURY

Wallwave set his mind to bury his young brother Stormbolt with naval honors in a longboat set on fire that would also carry away the loyal Whaleroarer.

Wallwave also wished to bury his uncle, Summersailor, who had gone to fight for Warchariot. For the Hillwolf King Warchariot had deserted the Summersailor and declared him to be a traitor and abandoned his body.

So Wallwave stood by his uncle Summersailor, since he also was a victim of witchery and deserved to go westward into the Isles of Youth where all great warriors had gone before.

King Wallwave was deliberate and dutiful, for deep anger and a great grief had come upon him when he had looked down upon the lifeless body of his young brother Stormbolt. He saw the brother who had been strong and skillful, loyal and honorable, become the victim of deceit, lies, madness and mind manipulation, now lying grey and cut off like a broken branch.

The Wallwave had been stunned when he killed Stormbolt. His mind had been struck frozen cold by the mask of death upon his brother's face.

Then personal servants carried the head and body of Stormbolt to the ship of the dead Whaleroarer. This ship was being prepared for the burning burial of a hero. The body of Stormbolt was carefully placed beside the shattered and broken pieces of Whaleroarer.

Then the Wallwave asked after the body of Summersailor and he was told it still lay cold upon the field of battle. For Warchariot and his War Queen

Snakeknife had refused to honor him or even recognize him as a comrade.

Snakeknife had ordered the body of Summersailor to be left dead and dry. Not to be desecrated, for the sake of the Hawkarmy, but not to be venerated because the body had been visited with bad luck. Summersailor in life had been a loser and only a doubtful friend of the Hillwolves, for a brief day of treachery. For such was the ruthless way of the Life of Win.

The hardblade Rainbowsword lay there beside the body of Summersailor. The sword was given, with all the other weaponry of the hero, to the Wallwave as a token of the former days of glory of Summersailor.

Wallwave asked his servants to bring the body of Summersailor to lie beside the body of Stormbolt in the burialship. For like his young brother Stormbolt, his uncle Summersailor had been deceived by all the lies and witchery of Warchariot and his grim and wicked War Queen Snakeknife.

So now in the ship of burial there lay the bodies of three heroes of the Seagulls: Summersailor, Whaleroarer and Stormbolt.

The loyal Maplewine refused to leave the bodies of the three great Wavewarriors and stayed on board to keep them company and steer the ship due west on its last voyage. The red and orange voyage was for a true hero. For the herolight shone all around the three dead Wavewarriors. That halo of fire and brightness still flashed around them. Even in death they had the aura of heroes.

War Queen Whitehair and her two remaining ladies, Streamflower and Willowflame were also stunned and silent and did not speak to the Wallwave. For what words could be said that would make any sense or what tears could be shed that would bring any comfort on such a day?

Wallwave laid the bodies and pieces and heads of Whaleroarer, the Summersailor and Stormbolt in a wide box and set it at the prow, raised up and looking forward. Then he set the sails and fixed the rudder to sail the boat to the west to greet the setting sun and travel home, far into the western Isles of Youth.

Maplewine cleared away from the funeral ship all traces and remains of everything except Stormbolt and his two dead companions sailing to the setting sun. The ship was put to flame. It burned with great red twilight clouds as it sailed into the sunset of the world.

Then a great wail rose up from the four winds and the voices of sea-drowned sailors wept in choirs to mourn for Stormbolt and his two companions from the fields of war. The oceans sighed in sorrow that they had been destroyed by lies and potions and cunning arts of shapeshifting and delusion from the black pit of mindmanipulation.

As the Wallwave looked at the burial ship, he spoke to all his fellow Wavewarriors.

"It is a shame upon me that there is left even one Hillwolf alive to tell the bitter tale of how, in anger and in haste, I killed my brother instead of the enemy. I wish that I had found an honorable death rather than this dishonorable victory. When we go to war, we go to war against our sons and brothers and daughters and our wives and not against our enemies alone."

Then a killfury rage came upon the Wallwave and he poured himself out upon the bitter foe, like the molten burning copper from a furnace, flowing into the cast of a weaponmonger, like a wallwave of the sea smashing on the shore.

When the Wallwave killfuried he came in his nightwrath suddenly and unexpectedly upon the camp of the unaware Hillwolves. Those Wolves who were asleep were awakened by the sounds of war; the smashing of shields splitting as the axes ripped through them; shouting and screaming; the crumble of spears and javelins; breaking bones; the roar of fires; screaming women and children; the yelping and howling of the dogs and cats.

The Wolves strapped on and fixed their combat armor and rushed into the battle expecting to find an army attacking them. Instead they saw a lone axeman in a killfury and one who fought like a hundred thousand warriors.

The Hillwolves were confused and stabbed at each other and ran around in circles to defend against only one man who had gone mad. And over the next few days the long killfury of the Wallwave roared and slaughtered on.

Then all the Hillwolf army came out in force. The regular soldiers and divisions were dressed in winepurple cloaks. Their hair was short; their knee-length tunics were of red and blue. Their full-length shields were bright silver and bronze. Each warrior carried his spear and javelins and wore a face and head mask of black wool.

The Hawk division were dressed in dark-gray cloaks, in calf-length tunics of lightblue like sky with thick embroidery of golden thread and in patterns and in circles and in pictures. Their spears and bunches of javelins were light for frequent and speedy use in the field of battle. Their head and face masks were of crimson wool.

The Wallwave stood on a cliff and spoke to all the grim assembled army of the Hillwolves, "May Deathfate come to you who stand against me. Deathfate also to those who help you fight but I wish good days to those you leave behind. I challenge you to come fight the Wallwave at any time of day or night you find me awake, or in my sleep, eating or resting, before my face or creeping up behind me."

***

Sly teams of killers were sent out by Warchariot and his wicked War Queen Snakeknife to find and surround and slaughter the Wallwave while he lay in his sleep. These killers were tense and quick-looking around, nervously jumping. As they prodded and poked in the jungle wastes, they found a small fastsleeping camp in the shadowy darkness and fell upon it and slaughtered every soul. Then they fled away and came back in the daylight to see if the Wallwave had been killed.

But once again the camp that they had murdered were only singers come from far off to tell tales of pastwars and sing the good oldsongs that had glorified the Hillwolves. All those singers and tellers of tales who had come to entertain and raise the spirits, had been killed by the Hillwolves, in their terror of the Seagull's Killfury.

For the hard and rigid mask and trance of death, in the cold morning light, had settled on those who had come to sing and storytell to the Wolves. And the Hillwolf blunderers wept and moaned in sorrow.

CHAPTER TEN
MINDMADNESS

Then the Wallwave sent for all his Seagulls to rally in the cove of a high cliff and he addressed the warriors in this way, "Too many of our comrades and our kinsmen have fallen before these lies and tricks and sorceries. Too many have been killed of all our friends by spells and shapeshifting, treacheries and delusions.

"These Hillwolves cannot fight without attacks on the minds and thoughts and souls of honest people. Therefore, I urge you all to follow me now with honorable swords and accoutrements of war. I will go out and slay a hundred of them on each and every day. I ask you only to keep the other thousands of their killers at bay and to keep them from throwing javelins at my back. So intercept those javelins and their spears with your own slings and shields.

"Form yourselves into a high guard along that ridge and cut off all their attempts to kill me from behind. If I am given a fair and honest chance, I will destroy all our grim enemies. I will slaughter them a hundred at a time."

Then the Wallwave stood high upon the ridge and shouted to the assembled hosts of Hillwolves, "I say that neither flesh nor bone can flourish from your tired army, except what may escape from the mouths and claws of the ravens that attack you. Send me a hundred warriors every day to this wide sandy bay to fight with me and I will dispatch a hundred of your dogs each morning, for you are all unworthy of any single combat on my part."

Then a great shout of contempt and arrogance, a vast cry of derision, roared from the Hillwolves. But they sent out a hundred men and chariots to meet Wallwave at the screech of dawn. And as the rooster crowed, Wallwave met them and poured himself out upon the hundred men like the molten burning copper from a furnace flowing into the cast of a weaponmonger. Like a wavewall of the seas smashing on shore, Wallwave slaughtered them in a torrent of red sword.

It was the longtime custom of the Hillwolves when they went into any battle for each man to lift up a granitestone and put it down nearby to form a mound. For each stone represented a warrior gone into the battle. When they returned from their hardfighting, each warrior carried away his own lifestone and the stones that remained were counted and totaled up. The stones that were left behind were the tally of the number of warriors who had been slain in combat, who never would return to carry away their lifestones from the mound memorial.

In this way, the remaining stones gave a quick number of those who had died in battle.

So the Wallwave called out to the one hundred, "Do not trouble to make a cairn for I will make one for you."

Then Wallwave made three separate mounds and piled them high along the ridge that overlooked the bay. One mound was made of weapons from the dead. One mound was made of bodies that had died. The third cairn was built up of severed heads of the grinning hundred who had been beheaded.

On the next morning he came ashore but there was no one to meet him. So he called out, "Find me a hundred or I will come and pick and choose my own one hundred favorites."

Then the Hillwolves got together and held a lottery under their King

Warchariot and his War Queen Snakeknife and they selected a hundred warriors to fight against the Wallwave.

The messenger of the Hillwolves begged Wallwave, "Give a few minutes for the losers in the lottery to write their wills and last wishes before they come to meet you." This was granted. And one hundred men were selected in the lottery of life and death and combat.

Once again Wallwave slaughtered all and made three mounds.

On the third day he killfuried.

King Wallwave wore a glittering, bluegray coat of mail and a purple tunic of fine woven ramswool. He held a silver and bronze shield of golden studs; two spears with sharp-pronged tips; a heavy sword with gems of gold and ruby glittering and ornamenting the cross-hilt. The Bonespear was in his hand as always; ready to leap out in eternal thirst for blood.

A black facemask of wool covered the head of the Wallwave and from his helmet sparkled four bright spikes. These were the four arts of the compass, shining like north and south and east and west, the symbols of his kingship over the waves.

Splendid and glowing like a golden warrior, his yellow skin reflected the dawning light. A herolight shone all about Wallwave. A halo of fire and brightness flashed around him.

He left behind his weapons in his chariot. Then he ran to meet the hundred chosen fighters with his bare hands and seized the nearest man by the feet. He swung the body like a sword to slay the nearest men. He killed them all, using live bodies like a young boy's bat and threw up three great piles of men and weapons. At the end of day a hundred bodies lay battered and dead as the deep sea came ashore.

Wallwave now returned to his own ships. And the hero, now as hot as molten copper, was plunged into a cold vat of icewater. He remained hot and breathing hard, but he was plunged again into a pool of cool sea water to calm down his head. Soon the cool water sizzled like a hot geyser. For a third time the Wallwave was plunged into a cold cauldron of brine and seaweeds. Only then did the water bubble to a mild warm.

Then a mindmadness came upon the Wallwave and he shivered and trembled but found no place to hide.

He gave his Bonespear back to the Icedragon along with the crown of brave Waterbear, his father.

The sharp-eared Shield of Roar that shouted warnings, these he gave to his top heroes and Whitehair but he retained the Rainbowsword that sent a rainbow high into the sky.

Wallwave tried to escape into the clouds or drown deep in the sea. Then the Wallwave fled to the great waterfall to join the voices, ghostily and madly swirling in the fountain.

Yet he could find no place where he could fly to; no perch upon the clifftops of the caves. And the Wavewarriors raised a great howl to help him, a huge shout of support for their great hero.

The Wallwave did not hear them shout because the spirits of the waterfall screamed louder. They cried "Join with us, join our ancient ghosts and hear our voices telling you what to do and where to go and what to think and see. Do not destroy us and we can live together. We are the dead of night, so come to join us. Let us all laugh and grin, widetoothly grins."

The Wallwave fought hardsword against the waterfall. As he warred with water demons and delusions, his sword flashed many colors of the rainbow.

Small birds and blustery squalls rose up to help support him against the grey long-bearded spout of endless water pouring from the rock. The birds knew well that the clean and whole Wallwave had tired and sickened of the witches' lies, their treacheries and unholy delusions, their images of false creatures from the pit.

But deeper voices from the wells of demons called on Wallwave to join eternal voices and stay with them forever in the pools. Yet fiends controlled the whisperings of deception and showed him cavalcades and splendid rainbows, lofty and slender streams turning around, spraying over the many colored rocks, spurting and splashing in cool refreshing beauty.

Voices of waterfiends spoke to the Wallwave, "Beware brave fighter of voices that misguide and try to entrap you in their caves forever."

So Wallwave fought with the demons of the waterfalls as the voices of the water made strange words.

"No more the time for war. No more the battle.

"War is the time for theft and kidnapping.

"War is the time for plunder and assassination.

"Why should you slash and cut off heads and limbs? Why should you killfury and destroy yourself?

"Isn't the sea around us still and isn't the earth under our feet, the sky overhead?

"So what has changed in all the world around us as a reward for all the cruel mayhem? The harvest of the combat is dead bones.

"Hold up your fingers, laugh and grin and count; naught through to nine. Witches' webs and demon faces and shapeshifting and projections and sea mists of forgetfulness and amnesias and lies and cunning plots and deceptions.

"Fly away to the snowy wastes and find a home among the birds and bears and seals and water fountains."

***

Then the War Queen Snakeknife congratulated King Warchariot, "Many hundreds and thousands have reached our camp. Heroes and champions and warriors have come and more and more are pouring back to us, now that the Wallwave has run away, now that the Wavewarriors have no more a leader."

Warchariot gloated and washed his hands with air.

"All the way several miles back I can see, where the fields and hills and forests used to lie, there is a moving mass of metal weapons, all in the hands of Hillwolves coming home."

More ships of the Hillwolves sailed in and they set their linen sails and built their blue awnings to protect them from the high sun and the spray, and they were served their fine wines and their stews of meat and vegetables. There they sat and listened to their pipers and their harpists. They heard their songwriters and their storytellers celebrate the deeds of war and conquest that would follow on if only they would pursue the fleeing Seagulls.

And the Hillwolves set up their revenge camp nearby. They arose early the next dawn, putting on their fine silk shirts, their ramswool blue and crimson woven tunics. The Hillwolves put on coats of brightest mail, shining beneath helmets of gems and gold, their purple and orange shields upon their arms. Their swords and spears and amulets and daggers were like colored feathers in the wings of roosters, swaggering and swaying and jerking up and down, all strutting cocks, crowing in the cold dawn.

For now the Hillwolves were coming back to strike against the Seagulls. Now that the Wallwave was not fighting a hundred at a time for his men but rather he was battling only against the demons of the waterfall.

The Hillwolves rose up like fighting birds of combat with the heavy harness of battle across their shoulders and they pursued the Seagulls to their death.

CHAPTER ELEVEN
THE OLD BATHHOUSE

While Wallwave fought with the ghosts of the waterfall, destroying the demons that screamed hatred at him, the Hillwolves never once dared to follow him in case he turned away from slaying spirits.

Yet the Hillwolves, encouraged by Wallwave's madness, threw themselves on the ranks of the Wavewarriors and tried to split the Seagulls into two parts.

War Queen Snakeknife ordered the Hillwolves, "Split up the foe and cut off the vanguard with their two great heroes, Icedragon and Stormleaper and their entourage. Drive them along the paths to the Old Bathhouse.

"I have made some improvements there, especially to help new visitors to take the waters. Those old steam spas are good for the spine and energy."

Warchariot washed his hands in invisible water.

As Stormleaper and the Icedragon whipped their chariots towards the coast, they saw the bathhouse.

Then War Queen Whitehair pointed towards the iron house, "We could make a stand there with all our camp. There is fire and water there. The walls are iron; a great place to defend if we are attacked."

She saw that the windows were well barred for use by archers and yet it did not seem to be heavily defended.

As the dozen Seagull chariots drove up, the four or five defending Hillwolves ran off.

The two grim heroes, Stormleaper and the Icedragon, dismounted, drew their swords and entered. The house was filled with empty cubicles for changing and holding clothes. Ranged all around were covered steambaths. Beside them were chairs, tables and mirrors.

An old dame in her nineties sat in one corner before a mirror. Two young servant girls attended her with combs and files and scissors and paint and makeup brushes. The room had some tables with fine fruits, candles and flowers.

The ancient lady pointed her finger at the heroes, "Do not dare to enter here. For this bathhouse is reserved for me, just now."

Stormleaper bowed low and then asked, "Who are you?"

"I am Queen Rainbow, mother of the Queen."

"You are the mother of the great War Queen Snakeknife?"

"I told you so. Get out or I will call her."

Then Stormleaper and Icedragon bowed and removed their helmets and walked backwards to the door.

Outside the bathhouse they spoke to their three warrior queens: War Queen Whitehair, Streamflower and red Willowflame, "We have a hostage. Go inside and bind her. She does not realize who we are. She is the ancient mother of the Snakeknife. Please be careful not to hurt her but do not let her escape."

The two young servant girls, who had been helping Queen Rainbow, came out with tubs of dirty water which they threw down the drain.

As Whitehair, Streamflower and Willowflame entered the bathhouse, the servant girls walked away. A short scream rang out as the old lady was seized and gagged and bound.

A few minutes later, some of their lookouts who had walked around the bathhouse, reported to Icedragon and

Stormleaper, "We have checked the bathhouse. Down in the basement smiths are stoking and filling the furnaces with coal and logs and branches. Their furnaces heat the water in the tanks below the baths. Steam rises through small holes into the air beneath the copper baths and the baths are honeycombed with holes for the hot steam to enter. Each bath is covered with a leather cape that keeps the steam in the bath. Servants control the flow of the hotair by pushing leather trays, backward and forward, underneath the baths.

"In the hot basement, the smiths are shoveling fiercely and fanatically as though expecting some clients of importance for the baths."

The Icedragon thanked the guards and answered them, "That may be so, for Queen Rainbow is here. Perhaps there are others of her house expected.

Let us go inside and close the great iron door."

Inside the iron house, when the door was closed, the Seagulls settled down to eat and sleep.

***

After a little while, Whitehair sat up and saw small bubbles crackling at the drains as it grew hot and hazy. She was puzzled and uneasy at this sight. She soon began to think of strange events.

In curiosity, Whitehair pulled off the gag plaster from the frail queen's mouth and asked the old lady, "Why did your servant girls never come back to help you after they had carried out two little tubs of dirty water?"

Queen Rainbow replied, "The dirty water flowed from the high steps down to the lower floor. It seems the drains recently became blocked."

Then Whitehair cried aloud, "Why did this Queen's small guard all run away? Waken up all. We are caught in a trap. The drains are blocked. The doors and windows likely are now locked!"

Stormleaper awoke and, startled by Whitehair's alarm, pulled back the curtains from the metal window, "Iron shutters." He cried, "What fools we are. The shutters and doors have been recast in iron and fitted tight. We are sealed."

Icedragon kicked and tore at the front door but only the wooden cladding came away and under the wooden surface was solid iron.

Icedragon cried aloud, "We are locked up and sealed inside an iron box, an oven that is slowly being heated and stoked up by six strong smiths and furnacers below."

Whitehair and Willowflame were now distraught. Streamflower began to weep and scream and beat on the iron walls. They jumped upon the tables as the bubbling water crept higher on the floor.

Queen Rainbow laughed. "My daughter is War Queen Snakeknife. When she finds that I am here in person she will order us released. Then you must fight to stay alive or she will surely kill you. She is a warrior Queen of many weapons."

Then Icedragon shook his head, "If Warchariot or Snakeknife had wanted a fair fight they could have had one and without all this deception and these contraptions."

"What do you mean? My own dear daughter, Snakeknife, would never let me die by your crude hands."

"You are not threatened by our hands," said Whitehair, "but by your treacherous daughter's hands. You need to know that you are not a hostage as I once thought. No, Queen Rainbow, you are a sacrifice and bait set for us to entrap us so that we can all be boiled or roasted alive."

"You are a Liar. If I am not a hostage then set me free."

"Do so now," Icedragon nodded to Whitehair.

Whitehair and her two ladies released Queen Rainbow who knocked her makeup box down the stone steps, where it rolled over and over.

Queen Rainbow ran to the great door and banged upon it, crying, "Snakeknife my daughter, this is your mother. This is your dear old mother, set me free."

Not a sound or answer echoed through the door which stood as immobile as a sheer cliff.

Queen Rainbow beat with her fists on the door and shouted, "Tell me, my daughter. Tell me if you can hear me?"

A clear voice on the outside of the door rang out. The fingers of the Icedragon tightened in anticipation on the Bonespear but the door remained as solid as a rock.

The voice of Snakeknife echoed through the iron door, "Be quiet mother or you will embarrass me before my warriors. They will think me ruthless. You cannot have long to live in any case and it is nice to die saving your daughter and my dear king and all our loyal men from the crude butchery of these Wavewarriors. Think of the greatest good of the greatest number. What better motherlove?"

Queen Rainbow wept and pounded on the door until at last she realized that she had been set up as bait to catch the Seagulls by her own daughter Queen Snakeknife.

"Murderous filth," she wept and called out. "You would slaughter your own mother to win a battle. Don't you know that those who murder their own mothers do not live long. Though I am old, I hoped for a long and quiet and serene retirement. How can you smash this hope?"

"Just think of me as a sudden heart attack that spoils your plans," said Snakeknife. "Even the best of us can have heart attacks."

Queen Rainbow smashed her fist against the door. "It's my fault, my fault for spawning you."

"Please do not blame yourself – such things are random."

Queen Rainbow moaned and bitterly fell silent, muttering, "Then you are random, murderous filth. Let all who would have children think of this."

Streamflower took the old lady and put her arms around her.

Then Willowflame said, "Come with us. Sit down beside your table on these steps for we will never harm you."

But Queen Rainbow was sick and trembling and, a second time, she dropped her dressing box upon the floor. It rolled over and over, through the hot and steaming bubbles that were building up, as the watery temperature rose high and higher.

"Look there," said Whitehair, "See that tumbling box and watch how it rolls over and over again. This old iron bathhouse also is a box. We are caught in a boxtrap. Why can we not make this big box roll over?"

"Just so," replied the Stormleaper, "If we could only roll this box down to the shoreline we could avoid the fires burning below us. Already this iron box is getting hotter.

"The steam is in the air, sweat on our brows. Hot water pours from small pipes into the tanks below the copper steam baths.

"If we can overturn this iron bathhouse with a great push the shock of being battered against the sides will cause us bruising, even some injury. So let us try this but with some precautions.

"Those cubicles of steel are strong and fixed to the walls and ceiling. Let Whitehair and her two ladies put their arms around Queen Rainbow and lock themselves inside a cubicle with the old one between them. This will buffer most of the shock of crashing this great bathhouse over the rocks that lead down to the sea.

"Also, pull out the small soft waterpipes where they pump the water into our tanks in case those small pipes might impede our effort to break away from the hot furnaces. Once we have overturned this bathhouse we know that they can roast but never boil us. I thank the powers of good for this small mercy."

The ladies locked themselves in the cubicle and the men hacked and broke off the small pipes where hot water trickled into the steam tanks. Some others tied down the furniture at the wall where they would throw themselves so as to add a little extra weight to their joint effort.

Hot water poured out from the broken pipes and hissed and bubbled on the heated floor.

Then the heroes and charioteers threw themselves hard against the wall with the piled-up furniture. The third time that they threw themselves against it, the wall buckled and bent under the weight of their combined assault. The bathhouse trembled, poised on its edge, then shook and tumbled over then the house fell flat on its wall side.

The enemy could see underneath there was revealed the open burning furnace with flames shooting high into the air. The smiths piled on and shoveled coal and wood, toiling like slaves to heat the old iron bathhouse. And so intent were they, they did not stop even when the bathhouse rolled over on its side.

When War Queen Snakeknife saw the flames from the furnaces leap high and send up clouds of billowy smoke she cried out loudly, "Stop it you fools. Save your fuel. Can you not see that you are heating the air?"

The men stood back, relieved and wiped their brows. Then the bathhouse crashed again and again as it rolled over and came to rest down on the rocky shore.

Warchariot strode upon the hillock crest and placed his arms akimbo and looked down. He ordered the master smith to kneel before him and drew his sword and asked, "Will your work stand?"

The master smith looked down, "No sign of life. The bathhouse may be moved but will never break. Nothing on earth will open it, my lord."

Warchariot and his War Queen Snakeknife laughed loud and long.

"Well," said Warchariot to the master smith, "Don't stand around and waste your time. Take all your men and move the faggots and tinderwood and pile the coal and logs against the old bathhouse. Set it afire. Perhaps it will take longer to roast that crew alive, rather than boil them. Even if the sea comes in to douse the fires, then slow starvation is the fate of many in this poor world, so why should they escape it? Or what if they should drown under the sea? The might of the Seagulls still would be abated."

***

Storytellers and singers came to report to Warchariot and Snakeknife on the other body of Seagulls who had been cut off from the group now trapped within the old bathhouse.

"They are weak and vacillating without a leader. And even as we speak those free Seagulls are being scattered abroad and cut to pieces."

Warchariot laughed again to hear this news and Snakeknife washed her hands with air and sneered, "Cut them or roast them, bury them alive just like the ones now trapped in the old bathhouse. Drown them, what is the difference? Come, let us call on these songwriters to celebrate our victory.

"So let us eat and drink and sing the songs and listen to the tales of how we triumphed. How fortunate we were to have my mother to bait the trap. Old fools will live forever if we don't stop them."

***

Inside the bathhouse the Seagulls crawled and creaked and stumbled from the crash but no one seemed to suffer but Queen Rainbow, who held her heart and gasped.

They all lit candles and searched the iron walls for cracks or breaks but found none.

"This is a fortress and a coffin," said the Icedragon. "I can hear outside the sound of digging. Soon we will be buried."

Then the great shield of warning began to shake and roared out a great cry of deadly danger. Even in the waterfall, the Wallwave heard but did not answer, for he felt compelled to fight the demons of the waterfall.

Then Queen Rainbow called the ladies to her side and whispered, "Goodbye. You saved my life, but I am old and cannot long survive this turmoil."

She took a chain and locket from her neck and gave it to Whitehair. "This is for all the ladies and warriors in this deadly cabin, for you were all entrapped here by my daughter. Here in this locket is the cameo of one I loved, long, many long years ago. Alas I left him, only to marry a king. Later my daughter was born, the offspring of a king and his bad blood. That daughter now is known as Snakeknife, the cold Queen of the Hillwolves.

"So take this locket. Open it when I die. Only this man I loved, in the locket picture, may still remember me and try a rescue. Only this man could save us from the Snakeknife. I am too weak to call upon him now. This is the one who has the power to save you."

When Whitehair took the small locket from Queen Rainbow she kissed the old one gently on the cheek. Then the old lady seemed to become young again and died.

Whitehair was distraught as she opened the little locket. Inside it was a picture of the face of a young Truthteller, whom she did not know. Whitehair wept in frustration and threw the locket against the iron door of the trap, in anger that the old lady had been speaking in riddles.

Suddenly a bright light flashed and filled the room. Then the door of the iron bathhouse flew wide open.

Truthteller stood there in the open space, tall and erect, wrinkled and gray of hair. He stepped forward, took Queen Rainbow in his arms and walked outside. Then he and the dead Queen disappeared into thin air as she was carried far, far away to the Islands of the Young.

***

The Hillwolves lurking outside, hoping to kill any of the Seagulls who escaped, were blinded by the bright appearance of the Truthteller. They covered over their eyes and ran away.

Then Stormleaper cried out, "See there. The Wolves have fled from the celestial darts of the Truthteller. Put on your armor and your shields of war so that when we burst out we will surely bring terror like a river bursting through its banks."

When they rushed outside they were indeed an ocean, flowing like a fierce fountain from a rock or like a molten fire, sparks flying high, out of a hill volcano, pouring down upon the plains.

Then the Icedragon, Stormleaper and the others took the Bonespear, the Shield of Roar and the crown of King Wallwave to the great waterfall to free Wallwave from his fight with all the demons of the waterfall.

CHAPTER TWELVE
RETURN OF THE WALLWAVE

When the Seagull Warriors flew out of the boilerhouse in their full armor of war, they were like birds flying from a falconer's cage.

The Hillwolves had already begun to celebrate victory and to eat, drink and be merry, for they had thought that the best Wavewarriors were dying in the sealed trap set for them; the old bathhouse of copper, iron and wood. Suddenly they all became terrified and scattered as the Seagulls poured themselves upon their enemy of both men and women.

But the taxrebels, who did not want to pay high tributes, joined with the brokenup platoons of the crack

Hawk division. They rebelled against their greedy and taxgrabbing King Warchariot and his evil War Queen Snakeknife. Also, they were repelled by their rulers' witchly friends. The rebels bared their swords at the great Hillwolf army.

Now that the Hawk army had no sworddeadly leader, now that the great Summersailor was laid low, the Hawks were free to join the disgruntled rebels.

The Hillwolves were hacked and hewed and some beheaded, for they were divided and splintered and not suspecting an attack.

Warchariot and Snakeknife fled to their own castle and held a council of war with the four witches to devise a plan that would confuse the foe.

But Meteoreyes looked far into the future and shook her head as she saw nothing there.

Then she spluttered out, "Alas, it is too late to plan. Now, here we are defeated and in flight from our fierce foes. This is the end result. This rout is the bitter humiliation of plots and spells and mindmanipulation. All we can do is to beg the powers of Win to reward us soon for our deep loyalty."

Then War Queen Snakeknife asked Warchariot, "Perhaps, if we had killed the Hawk division as I urged you at the time . . ?"

"Easier to kill King Wallwave," answered Warchariot, "The Hawks will not be sacrificed. Even now they and the taxrebels fight against our forces, shoulder to shoulder and in step by step, swords drawn and pointed towards our loyal Hillwolves. Fiercely, the way a mad dog bites a hand."

Mooncrow, in the shadows of the room, skulked there and croaked and shook off some black feathers. The Mooncrow cawed and crowed in the dark rafters, "There is a stranger in the washing room."

Warchariot and his Queen and the four witches stalked down to the basement of the landwolf castle.

There in the washing room sat a young woman with piles of pure white linen set before her. She rinsed the linen through a washing tub filled with clear water and then she wrung it out into a larger bathtub. As she did so, the rinsed water suddenly became a bright red crimson that was thick as blood.

The young Washerwoman began to weep and deep crimson tears were seen streaming down her cheeks.

Warchariot and Snakeknife and the four witches all shrank back in fear as a cold wind blew out the candles. When a servant lit up the room again, the Washerwoman and her pure white linen and red blood had vanished.

Then Snakeknife and Warchariot went next door and gave the orders for their evening meal. Silent and shiverly they stared in shock, brooding and wondering and then they returned above to their great council space high on the roof.

There the servants carried up their food and drink and placed it down before the King and Queen.

War Queen Snakeknife cried out, "Take this away, you fools. I asked for white wine but you bring me red. I asked for white fish but upon the plate I see red meat. So take all this away."

The servants took away the meal, begging for pardon. Again, a second time, they brought the meal and once again it had become red meat and crimson wine.

Warchariot became disturbed and rattled and fearful that even his own servants had begun to plot against him, anticipating a total destruction of the Hillwolves and a victory for the next ruler of the castle.

Again, he ordered away the meal in anger.

Then Warchariot leaned forward and touched Snakeknife's hand.

"Be calm, for these manifestations are not the work or the fault of our tried and trusted servantfolk. It is an omen from the other world."

And a third time the meal was changed and served with crimson wine and red meat of darkened blood.

War Queen Snakeknife was weak and shaky now, "I asked for white fish and for cool white wine but you must bring me red to rouse my blood. You disobey me. I will have your life."

The servant hid his face and answered, "This was white fish and white wine when we prepared it, but now that it has been placed before your majesties, it turns to red. We cannot understand it."

The meek servant moved aside his cowl and the King and Queen shrank back in a shivering of horror, for the man's head was a red skeleton dripping with blood.

The skeleton deathhead laughed low and muttered, "You cannot have my life for that light ceased a thousand years ago."

The skeleton then stood up and shook its robes and moved aside its cowl and grinned in mockery. "Soon you will both join us in a place of separation."

Then the skeleton apparition cried, "Come, come with us and join us soon," as it floated backwards, beckoning over the battlements of the castle.

Snakeknife arose and lifted up the table with the food and drink upon it as red as blood and threw it out over the castle walls to hit the skeleton. The sound of crunching bones was heard as the deathhead and the food and wine crashed down into the lapping waves below.

***

Then all the small critters, foxes, rabbits, dogs, cats, sheep and goats ran towards the higher ground.

When the good servants who were not enchanted saw all the small creatures run to higher ground, they also panicked and deserted. They took to the hills as, slowly and little by little, the seas rose.

But War Queen Snakeknife and Warchariot were defiant as they sat and brooded on the castle roof.

Then Warchariot muttered, "No mere blustery squalls will ever shake this castle. We have seen many storms since first the powers of Win placed us as chosen sovereigns on our throne."

But Snakeknife drew her hood around her head and curled within her cloak as the chill winds called all around.

***

Those cold winds and the rising tide of sea came from the Wallwave as he flexed his wings and rose up like an albatross over the sea.

For, after they had escaped from the iron bathhouse, the Stormleaper and the Icedragon had gone with Truthteller to the great waterfall to find their King Wallwave.

The shriveled-up demons of the waterfall had called out from the waters of the caves, "Now lie down and die Wallwave. You are mad. So cease to fight. Stop your wild slashing, stabbing and killcutting. Be wise and kind. Take your own life instead."

But the Truthteller had told the demons, "Be quiet. Tell no more lies, demons of the waterfall, for I am the Truthteller and my word is power. Your lies can only lead to self-destruction. You can survive only for a little while. Even now you and the waters must fall silent."

Then the Truthteller turned and spoke to the Wallwave, "Come King Wallwave, let us go back to your own Seagulls. Come with Stormleaper and the Icedragon and we will go back to Streamflower and to Willowflame and to Whitehair who has been devoted to you over so many years."

Voices of demons echoed away and silenced into the sky as they returned to the world where they belong. Demons disappear forever in the sunlight for they are powers of darkness and of night.

Then Truthteller and Stormleaper and the Icedragon led Wallwave back to camp nearby. Over the camp a dark cloud seemed to linger, just like the misty pall that drapes a palace when a king draws near to it on a winter's night. King Wallwave had come back to join his friends to think and repair his mind and pray to find wisdom.

The Wallwave curled up like an old cat going to rest in the nighttime, lying down and turning around, pawing about tiredly and quietly, head close to ground, twisting among the grasses to make a place for peace and for quiet contemplation. King Wallwave placed his weapons and accoutrements around him.

As he slept, his mind walked back into reality. His thoughts searched deeply among the greenscape of the mind, stepping tranquilly and pushing aside the shrubbery of delusion to find the paths that lead to a true wisdom. To find knowledge of what the gods want you to do and the courage to do it without the fear of man.

The Wallwave reached out all his hopes and fears to the old man in poor clothes, the one who had led the way.

Then he whispered. "Rule with us, Truthteller."

But the old man refused, saying, "The truth sets free but truth is neither a king nor ruler. I will advise and give my help to all who try to rule by conscience and by fairness."

After his rest, Wallwave came to his old self again. Like a cock crowing suddenly in the cold dawn he rose up like a bird and went to battle with the heavy harness of war across his shoulders.

Then he spoke once more to all the waiting Seagull Warriors. "I am still the Wallwave with the power to become a bird, powerful in shifting sands. I can stir up the earth and then the ocean beneath me as I fly over its waves and raise the sea like a curtain of despair. I can cause my friends to take the shape of Seagulls, for a short time, to save them from the flood; to save them from the greed and lust and avarice of futile wars, witchcraft, spells and potions. For all the weird shapeshifting of the witches cannot destroy the natural gifts of fate.

"So, become Seagulls and fly to our own castle. Go and lead and guide all our Wavewarriors to return home when they have killed our enemy. Guide home the Hawks back to our side once more and the new comrades who fled the heavy burden that once was paid in taxes to Warchariot and his wicked War Queen Snakeknife.

"All sail far out to sea, for I will soon become a mighty bird that threatens death to all beneath my wings. Soon wavewalls will rise up and sweep away all those beneath the wings of this great bird."

For three long days the wavewall tore and broke. It lifted up the earth and hills as it drowned the boats and houses and caves of the Hillwolves.

Then King Wallwave flew down to his boat with food and vials of water for the journey.

Floating in the swollen tide were the broken pieces of boats and homes and clothes and chariots and weapons and ploughs and farming tools – the flotsam of fear. There were many bodies of drowned men floating all around – the flotsam of death.

CHAPTER THIRTEEN
WATER OF LIFE

At last the party of King Wallwave with his War Queen Whitehair with her two ladies-in-waiting: Streamflower and Willowflame, the Icedragon and Stormleaper all flew down and changed into their human selves again. They flapped their wings and settled on the deck of their boat.

Leaving their magic forms as birds of prey, they took their places in the boat of war. As their boat sailed to the Castle of Warchariot they were joined in the swirling floods by the Truthteller.

They moored their boat alongside the great roof of the castle, for the seas had risen to almost cover the walls. Even now the waves licked high upon the ramparts so that the Wallwave could see what had become of the fort.

On the roof of the castle, Wallwave heard the voices of Warchariot and Snakeknife shouting in the drying air, "Give us something to drink or we will surely die."

Then the wild smallbirds of the Wallwave flew around in a circle, like a crown of mourning, like a flutter of mourners over a burial pit. Demons of destruction howled and screamed and the flotsam of the air swirled round about, circling the dread Castle of Warchariot. There, where the lives of many had been destroyed, smallbirds searched and sought for remnants or pieces of lost reminders of the dead.

Warchariot and his wicked War Queen Snakeknife cried to the Seagulls, "Three nights ago we had a visitation of blood-red omens telling of fatal nights and the waters have been rising ever since. We have had no drink or food since that dread day. These waters all around are from the sea."

Snakeknife began to weep and wail bitterly as Wallwave's boat drew close to the Hillwolf castle.

Kindly, the Wallwave spoke to the King and Queen, "I have vials full of drinking water here and I will give you some before my generals seize you and send you into a far exile."

"Yes," the Queen wept, "Let us have no more war. Let us go live in peace far, far away. Please also give us something to keep alive the four old women in the room below who think that they are witches with dark spells and potions. We will never plot again to murder or to deceive or to seize any lives."

But War Queen Whitehair spoke quietly to Icedragon, "No. I never will believe that lying woman again. Even Warchariot sees that the time for sham is past and gone."

Icedragon whispered quietly as he spread his hands and shook his head. "I know. But Whitehair, this is a decision for a king."

Suddenly a small dead bird floated alongside the boat of the Wallwave and his friends.

The old man in poor clothing pointed his hand at Warchariot and his Queen and spoke to them, "Funerals and vile finalities are all that you have ever brought to those you rule. Everything in your life is dedicated to helping you to climb high and stay aloft, looking down on your crawling pawns and peons. So now that you are high up, you should be happy."

At this point there was a flapping of dark wings and the Mooncrow flew past, she did not stop but fled alongside the flood, far, far away.

"Where that bird goes, ill days will live and flourish," said the Truthteller, still pointing at Warchariot. And as he spoke, the snow began to flake and flutter down.

The Truthteller spoke again, "This snow is like the Death Card in a cardpick. Snow speaks of Death or of a new beginning. King Warchariot and War Queen Snakeknife, you cannot know or try to understand that you are wrong. For you can see the world, and all things in it, only as a help or hindrance to your survival. You cannot see what may be good for others or what may harm them. You cannot speak truth or in your lives make any change for the better. Your future will be no different from your past."

Then Truthteller turned away from Warchariot and spoke to the Wallwave at his side, "Nevertheless if you have mercy in mind Wallwave, I will not advise against it. Mercy or no, you must decide, King Wallwave."

Wallwave closed his eyes as he replied, "I am not sure but I am of a mind to show them mercy, for to show mercy is the privilege and the honor of a king."

Wallwave took up a vial of drinking water then he stretched it out for Snakeknife to receive it across the rampart wall of the old fort from where he stood in his longboat of war. The dead sea lapped and rose up high between them.

Snakeknife reached out for the drinking water of life.

King Wallwave suddenly heard a mighty roar as a scene rose up before him of a combat, a vision that he had never seen before. It was when his uncle Summersailor had been slain by Stormbolt, younger brother of the Wallwave. Stormbolt had been dazed and deluded by false sights and voices woven in a web by the four Witches of Kill. They had been the hirelings and creatures of Warchariot and his War

Queen Snakeknife, who had planned the trap for Stormbolt.

Wallwave heard the shivering deathcry of the Summersailor as he had seized the javelin that pierced his throat and tried in vain to pull it out. Summersailor had sighed and fallen down into a pool of blood.

Then the sight of the Whaleroarer and Maplewine, as he had last seen them, came up before Wallwave. He saw their funeral ship sailing away on its last voyage, a blazing orange journey for the dead hero, while the herolight shone all around them, a halo of fire and brightness.

The other figures in the burning ship blurred in Wallwave's eyes, as he trembled and dropped the vial of drinking water into the sea. The sea of salt and poison and dead men and driedout birds; the black water rose and foully swirled between the boat and the fort.

Then Snakeknife wept and begged for a vial of water and once again Wallwave took up a vial of the drinking water and stood up in his ship and stretched it out for Snakeknife to receive it. And once again her eager trembling fingers reached out for the drinking water of life to slake the thirst in her parched, rasping throat.

Once again an image rose up before Wallwave that blurred his eyes and caused his hands to shake.

Wallwave saw clearly in front of him a scene that he had never seen before. For he saw that his father, brave Waterbear, had been laid in a ship, and ship and warrior had been set on fire and the steering fixed to sail far, far away to the Isles of Everlasting Youth.

Unseen by the others, his mother Queen Springvision runs to a crag overlooking the burning ship and leaps into the boat to join her husband King

Waterbear to be with him at last on his lone journey to the land of heroes.

When he saw this vision of his mother and father so burning away, Wallwave wept and trembled and dropped the vial of water into the sea, dead with dead bodies and the salt seaweed.

Snakeknife trembled and bit at her dry fingers and Warchariot cried out, "If you are a king worthy of any honor, give us the water, please. I beg you; give us the water to drink. Do not torment us with these cruel tricks. Let us go now into a far exile."

And a third time Wallwave took a vial of clearest drinking water and held it out for Queen Snakeknife to seize.

But now Warchariot pushed the Queen aside and held out both his hands to catch the vial, thinking that the Queen had not been deft enough to seize the vials that had been offered from Wallwave's hand.

Then, a third time, Wallwave saw before him a scene that shook him to the marrow bone, a scene that had taken place just days before. There, on the field of slaughter, bloody and smelling of death, Wallwave once again saw Summersailor but now, not far away, he saw the body and the severed head of his younger brother Stormbolt. The head cried out, "I died by the weapons of my elder brother, so let me be remembered for the one fight that surely turned the tide of battle."

King Wallwave, for the third time, his vision blurred with tears and his hand shaking, spilled the clear drinking water. But this time he did so deliberately and well before the grasping hands of Snakeknife or Warchariot could seize it from his firm grip.

For the Wallwave dashed down the empty vial into the sea, contaminated with the dead of earth.

Then King Wallwave cried aloud, with salt tears flowing down, "I cannot serve you. It is not in me, for a great rage rises up within me. You cry for water. Yes, you shall have water, more water than you will ever need in life. My mind is clear now. I am not in two minds. Justice is better than mere mercy. Mercy is for a day but justice stands like a beacon on the shore for many ships."

Then Wallwave took again the form of a whitebird and those around him flew up in the form of Seagulls. Wallwave spread his wings over the landwolf castle and blackened out the sun.

Then a savage storm arose once more in the sky below his wings. The dark clouds brooded and the waves leapt up and the mermaids screamed as their hair streamed out in terror. The smallbirds and the seabirds screeched in madness. The green seaweed waves were in an uproar as the seas rose up in anger and in hatred and the mindless hovering birds attacked each other.

And the great Wallwave rose over the castle once more and crushed all of the life of the King Warchariot and his wicked War Queen Snakeknife.

The witches squirmed in fear and spoke their spells. They drew around them visions of false creatures designed to swim or fly and carry away the witches on their backs to escape the Wallwave.

But these delusions, creatures of the pit, vain mandolphins and cold flamebreathing dragons, would neither swim nor fly in the sky to safety. So the witches frozen by their own magic crawled and cringed in their corner into dead and static icelike statuettes. They watched the water seep into their room, rising up higher and higher to endrown them.

Then the blasphemy and lies and mirror images out of the pit of everlasting torment and all the man-beast creations of the witches and all their crude spellsheets, were churned and battered as they were slowly submerged in the wallwave's waters.

So all those who had planned and plotted the wars and murders, the wicked War Queen Snakeknife, her husband King Warchariot and the old women who were the four Witches of Kill: the Windweasel, the Rivershark, the Landslink and the Meteoreyes were swept away with all the crawling filth of their shapeshifting.

***

Then the Wallwave folded his white wings and flew down and regained his boat.

And the old man in poor clothing, the Truthteller, went back to seek new wisdoms and good works and to read the books in his celestial study.

Whitehair, tall and stately as a swan of winter snow ready to switch its wings and fly to summer, sailed with King Wallwave to his castle with all the Seagulls.

Then Streamflower of the floating waterlilies and Willowflame like a burning willow tree and their two heroes returned once more to the Castle of Wallwave.

There Stormleaper and Icedragon became the two strong arms of the Seakingdom that was set among the high wallwaves of the Seaempire.

There King Wallwave reigns and rules today. But one day, it is said, he will fly again.

The End